I0557196

Broken
By
Truth

By

Dr. Jeri Fink

And

Donna Paltrowitz

Photography by Dr. Jeri Fink
Cover and book design by Derek Murphy

Broken By Truth
Written By Dr. Jeri Fink & Donna Paltrowitz
Photographs By Dr. Jeri Fink
Book and cover design By Derek Murphy

Published By Book Web Publishing, LTD
Copyright © 2016 By Jeri Fink and Donna Paltrowitz
All Rights reserved

ISBN: 978-1-941882-04-7

No part of this publication may be reproduced, stored in or introduced into a retrieval system, or transmitted, in any form, or by any means (electronic, mechanical, photocopying, recording, or otherwise), without the prior written permission of both the copyright owner and the above publisher of this book.

For Vinny,
who showed incredible love, courage, and dignity in his fight for life.
Our love to Ricky, Sheldon, and God's Love We Deliver –
they were always there for Vinny.

As promised, Vin, this book is for you.
Rest in peace.

Check out more *Broken* books written by Dr. Jeri Fink:

Broken By Truth

Broken By Birth

Broken By Evil

Broken By Madness

Broken By Kings

Broken: The Prequel

To Purchase books go to: hauntedfamilytrees.com/books

or amazon.com

Is there a psychopath in your life? Go to http://hauntedfamilytrees. com/ haunted-family-trees-landing/ to sign up for your FREE copy of Dr. Fink's ground-breaking guide.

Discover the secrets of haunted family trees – from the infamous to your own Go to: http://hauntedfamilytrees.com/ haunted-family-trees-landing/ to get stories that will amaze you, the truth in facts and photos, and the latest info about family curses and bizarre behavior.

Do you love photo insights? Go to: http:// hauntedfamilytrees.com/ landing-page to get a free image each week in your email that will enlighten, inspire, and make you feel good.

Broken
By
Truth

PRESENT DAY

Dr. H

1

It began with the perfect idea.

Truth With Dr. H! was a hit TV tabloid show.

Ratings soared and the credit was *mine* – the freshest voice to emerge in media psychology. It didn't matter that I just turned 66. I was the next generation to reveal great truths about the human condition – an ageless baby boomer. You could follow me on broadcast, cable, or online; watch the *You Tube* clips that spread like a pandemic, or read my book, *Truth With Dr. H!: The Real Story* as a hardcover, paperback, or ebook. Some downloaded the audio version and listened, mesmerized while they drove, exercised, or commuted. For the most loyal fans, there were refrigerator magnets, tee shirts, tote bags, and the ubiquitous "H" pendants forged from 100% recycled plastic water bottles.

Fans were captivated. Guests were discussed, issues argued, and there was an ongoing dispute over *who* were the villains and heroes. The debates reverberated in clubs, dive bars, posh restaurants, and at family dinner tables. Social media was swamped.

Everyone had an opinion.

Critics described the show as unscripted drama with a dollop of *true* psychology – Dr. Phil, Oprah, and Springer rolled into one lip-smacking format. Late night TV hosts alluded to us in their opening monologues. Viewers saw themselves in our good, bad, and evil guests. The angle was simple.

Truth.

Good old truth. We love it, hate it, and play with it. At best, it's slippery – elusive – different for each of us. I believed it all until that infamous moment, taped live for national TV, changed everything. After that, *my* truth was never the same.

The *Perfect* Idea, as usual, emerged magically from the calculating minds of tabloid TV producers. It was designed to enhance the brand – make me more prominent on social media sites like Facebook, Twitter, and Reddit. If Anderson Cooper, Lady Gaga, and Justin Bieber could have millions of followers, couldn't I?

My face, with wide brown eyes and tightly controlled curly hair, was on commercials, print ads, and pop-ups. *Entertainment Tonight*, *TMZ,* and CNN covered me along with the hottest celebrities of the day. I was seen and heard everywhere. I *loved* the role. I grinned at the camera and shrugged off the shadows – forgetting that the wolves were always waiting.

No one in my family escaped them.

Human camps were shadowed by wolf packs over 150,000 years ago. Inevitably, some wolves learned not to be afraid of the strange, two-legged creatures. Those individuals wandered into the camps and were domesticated; evolving into the species we call dogs. Outside the glow of campfires, the wild wolves remained predators – looking and sounding like dogs, but very different in nature.

The wild wolves in my family were psychopaths. We were paired in time by forces no one could identify. God? Satan? Coincidence? Our pasts crossed over and over again, spanning five centuries. The psychopaths needed us to continue their legacy of broken souls. Kabbalists called it *gilgul* – the recycling of souls – returning over and over again, repeating the same horrors in a different context.

Did we need the wolves, as well?

Despite my *Francis Klein* handmade glasses from France, *Noritake* gold trim china tea cup, and embossed parchment letterhead, wolves stalked The *Perfect* Idea.

I couldn't escape them.

2

My production team ran with The *Perfect* Idea. I had several teams. Each followed specific themes. We were all seasoned New Yorkers, requiring philosophy to justify behavior. No one played the role of an empty-headed Hollywood blonde. We claimed to be above power and money, immune to greed, and in awe of truth.

We were skilled at deluding ourselves.

The *Perfect* Idea was no exception. It fit neatly into my rationale that each theme reflected the ultimate postmodern truth. "In postmodernism," I explained repeatedly, "the only *absolute* truth is that there are no absolute truths."

Cute.

It made my show easy to design. Almost anything fit within that definition. *Truth* could be found wherever one looked. We often carried truth to the extreme, nestling it safely in viewer illusion. People loved it.

Is your ex-boyfriend in jail really the father of your baby?
Did your mama cheat on your papa?
Is your toxic lover having an affair with your best friend?

There was always someone who fit the bill – a "guest" willing to exchange dignity for 15 minutes of fame. Finding people was never a problem.

I remembered the brainstorming that led to The *Perfect* Idea that changed my life.

"We have to do something *big*," I said to my production team. We sat around a large, elegant bamboo conference table with a platter of colorful raspberry macarons.

They were the best in the city.

We clutched personalized mugs of caffeinated hazel nut coffee and called out questions. Griet Vansalee, my executive producer, stood in the corner of the room and observed.

"Do you want to find out your baby's *real* father?"

"Did he get you pregnant and then demand an abortion?"

"Why can't you say *no* to your abusive lover?"

"What happened to the baby he made you give up?"

There was no end to the ideas. Everyone had problems and secrets; every family seethed with conflict; each of us was immersed in crime, whether real or perceived.

The postmodern id had gone viral.

3

The last question stuck. We expanded it.

Were you pressured to give up your baby by an abusive lover and now want to find out what happened?

It worked. Viewers loved to hear tragic stories of cute babies and wide-eyed abandoned children. Those truths were as popular as cheating lovers, spouses with secret families, and intimate betrayals. This idea had both.

The next step was to find stories. The question was posted on the *Truth With Dr. H!* website. *Respond by email if you're interested in telling your story.* I made requests during the show and taped an announcement that appeared between commercial breaks. The words were blazed onto a vivid blue screen and paired with heart-thumping background music.

Were you pressured to give up your baby by an abusive lover?
Were you too young to make the decision to defy him?
Do you ever wonder about what happened to your child?
Contact us. You can tell your story on *Truth With Dr. H!*

The staff went to work, sorting through stories, telephone calls, and videos. We were inundated with responses. Bookers poured over names and lurid tales, interviewed prospective guests, and debated who would be best for ratings. Eventually, two gripping stories were selected, 53 year old Moeda and her daughter, 37 year old Ayla.

Moeda, in a throwback to relatives from 17th century New Amsterdam, used the corrupted Dutch word for mother. She never wanted people to call her Ayla's mommy. She changed the spelling from Moeder to Moeda because she thought it was cool. That was very important in 1976 when Ayla was born and Moeda was still a teenager.

Sixteen years later, Ayla ran away from home to be with her fierce, 52 year old biker boyfriend, Mack. Mack battered his teenage lover, forcing her into becoming his sex slave and servicing gang members at his request. Ayla happily obliged. Things went sour when Ayla got pregnant and said nothing until it was too late for an abortion. Mack couldn't beat the kid out of her. She gave birth to the biker's baby and abandoned her child when he was one day old. Mack had given her an ultimatum – *me or the kid.*

Ayla, also a child, saw no other choice.

Moeda didn't find out about the baby until Ayla showed up at her house, 18 years later. Ayla was tired of her now-white-haired boyfriend. Even the fierce tattoo of the Nazi Iron Eagle covering his chest was sagging in aging male breasts.

It was a tearful reunion between mother and daughter.

Moeda and Ayla both wanted to find the abandoned baby. He was an adult now – around 21 years old. Ayla confided that she gave him a name – Joshua.

"Biblical Joshua was born a slave and later became Moses' military commander," Ayla explained. "He was a spiritual and military leader who lived to 110 years old. If my Joshua is like that, we *will* find him."

Moeda grieved the loss. "I have a grandson to love, but I don't know where he is."

"That's what I wanted for my son," Ayla pressed, "life, love, and respect. All the stuff we never got. I left a note with him . . . I don't know if they changed his name."

Moeda had her doubts. Anyone who had to wrestle with abandonment and the foster care system didn't have much of a future – which was why she never gave up Ayla for adoption.

Regardless, Mother and Daughter set out to find the baby. Neither knew how to negotiate the system. They hit brick walls wherever they turned. When they heard Dr. H's request, it seemed like an ideal solution. They applied and my producers found them.

It was the perfect story – guaranteed to boost ratings.

I approved everything.

4

Moeda and Ayla eagerly accepted the offer to appear on *Truth With Dr. H!* They were given a night in an exclusive Manhattan hotel, hair and make-up do-overs, and the opportunity to tell millions of people that they were searching for an adult male who was abandoned at birth.

It was too good to be true.

Ayla told us that she fantasized her child was a rock star manager, doctor, or prominent businessman.

Moeda was more realistic. "If he grew up in a good family," she mused during an early interview, "perhaps the child finished college. If he grew up in foster homes . . ." She shook her head and sighed, not having the heart to finish the sentence.

Excitement and optimism pervaded their visit. They couldn't wait to address the country. Someone *had* to know what happened.

Secretly, the team was instructed to search for Ayla's ex-73 year old boyfriend, Mack, the father of Ayla's abandoned child. He was to receive an invitation and ticket to the show. We held a team meeting to script the scene.

"There will be real shock on Ayla's and Moeda's faces," I commented, "when Mack rises from a strategically-placed seat in the center of the audience. Drama, my friends, that can't be scripted."

Tabloid TV thrived on that kind of scenario. We all knew the game – boos and cries of horror surge like an emotional tsunami. Mack would approach the stage, sit next to me, opposite the women, and sparks would fly. Security would be alerted. After all, Moeda had never met, face-to-face, with the man who had stolen her daughter.

With luck, someone would call in with information. Or better, maybe the abandoned child would contact us and appear on a follow-up. Either way, the show would be a hit. Ratings would soar.

I could bank on it.

5

The show began in the usual way.

The staff instructed Ayla and Moeda on TV etiquette and unexpected behavior. Others tended to final touches on my hair, make-up, and smoothing wrinkles from my face and cream-colored Armani suit.

Fresh roses were artfully placed in a vase. I needed flowers on the stage, honoring Jewish organizer, activist, and advisor to presidents, Rose Schneiderman. In 1911 she said, "the woman worker must have bread, but she must have roses, too."

I knew how Rose felt, except I needed *all* flowers, not just roses. I thought of the *Macy's Annual Flower Show* – an event I never missed. The store was decorated with incredible blooms, in brilliant colors and scents, heads bobbing like my studio audience.

I looked at my audience; the cluttered studio was filled to capacity. They were mostly women, with a handful of men and a small, mixed group of college students. In the center was a white-haired man, with sagging muscles, tattoos, and a flat, expressionless face.

Mack.

Griet pointed him out. "He's here."

"I know."

She nodded. "It's going to be quite a show."

"It always is."

The staff began the warm-up. Jen, a chubby associate producer, dressed in too-tight jeans and an oversized orange Dr. H! tee, danced seductively. She shook flabby hips and made gestures that drew smiles from the audience. Mia, a wiry blonde, leaped onto the stage, dressed in high boots, denim mini shorts, and a fitted Dr H! tee that showed her nipples. She imitated Jen's movements and the audience laughed. Shane appeared with a mike and broad smile. His dark hair highlighted piercing blue eyes; his muscular frame was displayed in tight leather pants that outlined his genitals.

"What do you think of our dancers?" He wiggled, yelling into the mike.

There was a smattering of applause. One young woman raised her fist.

"Are they the real thing?"

A few people cheered.

He thrust his hips at the audience as pounding music filled the studio. "People," Shane demanded. "Are you awake? Let's hear you scream."

A few raised their arms and voices.

"Everyone," Shane ordered, "stand up."

The entire audience obeyed except for Mack. The music got louder. "Dance," he said, waving his arms and moving his body as if in a porn movie. "I want to know. Is this CNN? MSNBC? No! It's *Truth With Dr H!* Are you ready for truth?"

Everyone cheered.

"Louder!" Shane shouted, grinding his hips faster. The girls on stage screamed, the audience mimicked them.

"We want noise. Lots of it."

There was pandemonium.

"I want to welcome our very own Dr. H!"

I breezed onto the stage, facing an audience that cheered me as if I were a rock star. I smiled humbly as a six-foot high flat screen flashed still images of me with my most notorious guests: mothers of serial killers, lovers of death row inmates, women who stabbed abusive husbands and got away with it.

The music roared. The studio was designed to be loud – magnify audience sounds against the heavy equipment, cameras, lights, and hard floor.

The white-haired old man didn't react.

"Welcome!" I shouted into the mike. "We're here for the truth."

There was a roar of *wahoos*.

I paused, smiling demurely. "Thank you, friends. We have a great show today with real truths."

I stared into the dark sea of faces.

Once, I thought of myself as the ugly duckling, growing up in the bland mythology of Long Island. Now, in front of my audience, I was a graceful, lone swan basking in the spotlight.

Dedicated to truth.

The audience settled, music muted, and I continued in my most compelling shrink voice, strolling up the center aisle and pausing in front of quirky individuals seated on the end for that purpose.

"Do you want the truth?" I asked an angry-looking woman, shoving the mike into her chubby face.

"Do you want the truth?" I asked a 20-something dressed in jeans and a skimpy shirt that highlighted a bony, sexless chest.

"Yes!"

I made my way through the audience and in a dramatic swirl, returned to the stage.

The six-foot screen went dark. The music died.

"Sit," I commanded, God-like.

The audience sat.

I hovered in front of my thickly cushioned brown leather chair – a few inches higher than the two chairs opposite it. I stared into the camera, softened my stance, and spoke to the red light that indicated it was taping.

"Today," I paused, taking a deep, audible breath, "we're going to meet two women. A mother and her daughter. The mother wants to meet her only grandson, but the daughter abandoned him a long time ago. Now they both want to know what happened to the child."

The music grew tense like a sound over in a horror flick. The screen flashed words that vibrated against black.

I abandoned my baby. Now I want to know where he is.

I paused. The audience was very still.

"It's time," I shouted, "for truth."

6

The audience was mine.

"Let me introduce Moeda," I said gently, emphasizing *introduce*.

The flat screen burst into life. Staccato images flashed – teenage Moeda, a political intern, and a mother with her infant. It paused on Moeda today.

"I want to meet my grandson," the image on the screen said soulfully. "I never knew he was born. My daughter ran away and until three years ago, I had no idea he existed." Tears coursed over her cheeks in a tremulous digital glow.

The audience moaned with compassion.

"Moeda," I raised my hand in a welcoming gesture. "Please join us."

Moeda walked nervously onto the stage, her eyes scanning the crowd. She wore a white shirt tucked comfortably into classic black pants with a thin *Salvatore Ferragamo* leather belt.

The audience was still.

"Moeda had a daughter named Ayla," I said softly. My voice coach had shown me how to emphasize the critical word. "She *ran* away.

I exhaled noisily and lay my hand over my heart.

"Moeda," I continued theatrically, "tried desperately to contact her daughter but the child refused to come home. She threatened her mother – told her that her biker boyfriend would kill her if she didn't leave them alone. Moeda said she would contact the police – get the boyfriend arrested for statutory rape. Ayla said that her boyfriend was a man of many means – the leader of a notorious biker group. If *he* couldn't kill her, someone else would."

Heads in the audience nodded in sympathy. The camera switched to them and then back to me.

"Three years ago," I raised my voice, "Moeda's daughter came home. It was a tearful reunion. Like all good mothers, Moeda welcomed her child unconditionally. She didn't ask questions. Eventually, Ayla told her story. A long time ago, Ayla had a baby with her biker lover. He forced her to give up the child and run away with him. The newborn was abandoned at a police station and the two fled on his motorcycle, protected by his deadly gang."

I waited for the story to root in the viewer imagination.

"Now," I thundered, "Ayla has won Moeda's forgiveness. Together, mother and daughter want to find the baby."

The crowd roared.

Pale-faced, Moeda stared at the audience – a deer caught in the headlights.

The audience jumped to their feet and cheered. Moeda forced a weak smile.

"I want to introduce Ayla, Moeda's daughter. She ran away with her boyfriend – when she was 16 and he was 52 years old!"

The monitor flashed wildly with images of Ayla – a baby, a toddler, a little girl dressed up in a school play, and an awkward teenager. A short video of Ayla's 16th birthday played across the screen. It ended with Ayla today, a 37 year old woman who looked closer to 50, her caramel-colored hair thin and disheveled, blue eyes dull, and her nose crooked, as if once broken and never properly healed.

"I made a big mistake and hurt many people," the image said slowly. "And now I want to fix it."

The audience booed – some waved their fists, others shook their heads angrily.

"Ayla," I said sternly, "come join us."

Ayla walked onstage, looking much better than on the screen. The audience jeered louder. A few young women hissed as if she were a villain in an old silent movie tying the heroine to the railroad tracks.

I pointed to the chair and Ayla sat. I turned to the audience and caught the gaze of the white-haired man in the audience. He was rigid.

"Wait," I cajoled the audience in a hypnotic voice. "Ayla was only 16 years old when her baby was born. And Mack, her boyfriend, forced her to abandon the child. She was only a child herself."

There was dead silence.

"Why didn't you tell me?" Moeda demanded.

"I was scared that he would kill you," Ayla retorted.

"And now," I continued, "Mother and Daughter, reunited, want to find out what happened to that baby."

The audience cheered wildly.

"Sit," I commanded.

7

"Why?" I settled into my chair and confronted Ayla.

"I was a kid," Ayla whined. "I did everything *he* wanted."

"Is that why you abandoned your baby?"

"I didn't know any better. Mack said he would leave me – kill me and the baby – if I didn't get rid of it. He would kill my mother if I said anything. I knew he could – or get one of his biker gang guys to do the job. They *loved* blood."

No one moved.

"And there was the cat."

"The cat?"

"I called him Baby – a caramel-and-white feral cat that I fed in our apartment. We got attached until Mack saw, slipped out his *hunter* combat knife, grabbed Baby and ripped open the cat's belly in one seamless motion. Blood spurted everywhere as the creature shuddered and died, never making a sound."

The audience gasped collectively.

"You see, Mack and his followers didn't care. Mack was the leader and they did what he said. Murder was like having breakfast. They all had guns and knives – all had killed many times before. To get into the gang you had to murder at least one person, usually homeless, drunks, or junkies. They did what Mack told them or got killed themselves. It was very simple."

"They scared you?"

"I was terrified and very obedient. Mack asked me to do . . . sex things . . . I never argued. He loved to watch . . ."

The audience froze.

"Sex things?"

Ayla hung her head.

"Did you . . . pleasure them?"

"Only when he asked," she whispered. "With my mouth."

"Often?"

"Too often. Mack didn't care. He said I was his sex slave and he lent me to them."

"What if you didn't obey?"

Ayla lowered her head and mumbled something no one could hear.

"What?"

"He beat me. Raped me."

"How can a man rape his girlfriend when he was already having sex with her?"

"He didn't listen when I said "no." It hurt and he didn't care."

I nodded.

"It wasn't always that way," Ayla added. When I was good and did exactly what he said . . ." Her voice drifted.

"Why didn't you run away?"

"Where?" Ayla raised her head defiantly. "Home? I was in love with Mack. I figured that he had me do those things because he loved me. After, he was gentle and loving most of the time. So I didn't mind it *that* much."

I shook my head, letting her words sink into the audience collective. "I have a very important question for you," I said finally. "The way you answer it might give you a clue about who your baby is today as these things sometimes run in families."

Ayla took a deep breath.

"Would you say," I spoke slowly and deliberately, "that Mack is a psychopath?"

Ayla looked at me blankly. "What's a psychopath?" She knew the answer but had been prepped to pretend she had no idea what I was asking.

I was ready.

"In the early 19th century," I explained professorially, "the word *psychopath* described a person who was normal on the outside and morally depraved on the inside. Today, many people think of a *psychopath* as someone who murders without feeling and *sociopath* for those who have no feeling. Essentially, both are callous and uncaring, with a total lack of empathy. They have few or no emotions, blaming others for things that are their fault – often using language that cons people into believing their lies. The psychopath who murders a stranger on the street might explain his behavior by saying, 'He or she (the victim) made me do it.'"

I paused, giving the audience time to absorb my words.

"They're often overconfident – grandiose, impulsive, self-centered, and unable to plan for the future. They lie, manipulate, and wreak havoc on those around them. They don't care about *you*. Many are violent – abusive – and have no tolerance for frustration. Some are charming, glib – able to fake love for blood. They can hurt, maim, and kill without a care in the world."

"Mack?" Ayla whispered.

I nodded. "They have no regard for life. Their brains are wired differently. Authors and filmmakers love them because they look human and sound human, but are missing what many of us call souls. One psychopath, linked to nearly 20 murders, described getting a "rush" every time he killed someone. 'I like to watch their eyes as they die . . .' he said."

The audience squirmed.

"In the movies," I continued, "there's Hannibal Lecter, Freddy Krueger, and The Joker. On TV, crime shows love to feature murdering psychopaths – serial killers and rapists – that terrify viewers. In real life, we know the names from the news – people like Adam Lanza who killed 26 children and adults in Newtown, Connecticut; James Holmes who shot and killed 24 people in a Colorado movie theater; and Ariel Castro, who imprisoned, raped, and beat three young women for 10 years.

Ayla wrung her hands, twisting them over and over until everyone noticed. The camera zoomed in.

"Each day, the list grows longer." My words reverberated in the ensuing silence.

Ayla trembled.

"Now I ask you the question again. Is Mack a psychopath?"

"Of course Mack's a psychopath," Moeda screamed. "Can't you see that?"

"He loved me," Ayla said softly. "My father – who I never met – didn't love me. Mack did. That means that Mack could *feel* – he wasn't a psychopath."

"Even when he beat you?" Moeda stood up and towered over Ayla who cowered in her shadow. "Is that feeling?"

"Please," I cajoled, "stay seated."

Moeda sat. "Why didn't you get an abortion? It was legal. You weren't that stupid."

"It was too late. I didn't have money. Mack tried to beat the baby out of me but it didn't work."

"Why didn't you ask Moeda?"

"I was afraid. And angry."

"Angry at what?"

Ayla glanced at Moeda. "How she raised me."

"Is that the whole story?"

"Yes, that's the whole story," Moeda interjected.

"Did your mother beat you?"

"No."

"Did she psychologically abuse you?"

"No."

"Then why did you run away?"

"I was young. It takes more than a check to raise a child. I fell in love with Mack. He was like . . . a father figure. I never had a father – a man – in my life. It was only me and Moeda."

"How did you live?"

"Moeda took money . . ."

"Did she steal it?"

"No!" Moeda shouted. "I never stole anything.

Ayla evaded the question. "Moeda hated Mack. She knew about the Nazi Iron Eagle tattooed on his chest and the lightning bolts on his leg pointing to his . . . penis."

The audience collectively giggled.

"Didn't *you* know better?"

"No. I thought I met the love of my life."

"And now?"

"He's an old man, Dr. H. He's disgusting."

"Is that *truth*?"

"Truth? He was always disgusting," Moeda railed. "You just never saw it. For God's sake, Ayla, he's older than *me*."

"He wasn't always disgusting,"

"He hit you. He raped you. He tried to beat the baby from you . . ."

"Not exactly . . ."

The audience went wild.

I didn't try to stop them. Angry voices and catcalls filled the studio. I waited for the noise to die down. Something caught my eye. I glanced at the white-haired man in the audience. Mack. I could see an icy blankness in his eyes. It was a familiar look that sent chills down my back.

Mack slowly rose from his seat. No one noticed – all eyes were on me, Ayla, and Moeda. He raised a white plastic gun and took aim. I thought it was a toy gun. There was no time to scream, to act, to take *any* action. His white hair shimmered beneath the hot lights. A shot blasted through the cramped studio, reverberating off lights, cameras, sound equipment, and booms. For an endless moment, no one moved. Blood spattered Moeda's white blouse. Her eyes widened in confusion. Blood sprinkled my cream-colored Armani suit.

Like red polka dots. Definitely in style.

The audience screamed and stampeded for the exit. People fell, others were trampled. Mack disappeared in the chaos as Moeda slowly slipped to the floor.

8

The cameras taped me, Moeda, Ayla, and the stampeding audience. The booms picked up screams, cries for help, and security struggling to control the hysteria. It was pandemonium. I didn't know where to look or who to help. I touched the blood on my Armani suit and it smeared like raw meat. A bizarre voice cackled in my head.

This is great footage.

NYPD was alerted. Ayla kneeled next to her unconscious mother as Sage, my grandniece and graduate student intern, rushed to the stage.

"Are you okay?" Sage begged, grabbing my arm.

I stared at her wild red hair and hazel eyes.

"I'm fine."

"The hamsa," she whispered, "is burning."

"I don't understand," I said sharply. "How the hell did he get through security?"

The cameras continued to roll. The red light winked at me as if in warning.

Definitely great footage.

I knew the answer. He was invited – *we* brought Mack into the unscripted drama.

"Cry," Sage whispered in my ear. "Everyone is watching."

I forced tears, then sobs, trembling like a dog on the way to the vet. Was it show for the camera? Or truth? Was there yet another set of truths invading my life? Something metal crashed to the floor and people screamed louder, pushed harder, fighting to get out exit doors already jammed with bodies. It was insanity – panic – a horror scene from the big screen.

Sage gathered me in her arms. She was a doctoral student doing an internship in media psychology; and my precious grandniece and dead sister's grandchild. She was the wearer of the family hamsa – an exotic blue-and-silver charm with "eyes" to protect against the evil eye. It was supposed to bring good luck.

Sage, only 23 years old, knew instinctively what to do. Maybe that was her good luck? I followed her instructions.

"Raise your arms, Hanya. Tell them to stop."

"They won't hear."

"It doesn't matter. The cameras will."

I took a deep breath and steadied myself. My voice was shaky but strong. "Stop – everyone will be okay if you stop."

No one heard but the cameras.

I stepped off the stage and wrestled with people at the back of the crowd. "Stop. Calm down. Please. Everything will be okay."

It was useless.

It wasn't until the police arrived that people began to settle. The cops knew what to do. Injured were dragged from the mob, frenzied leaders immobilized, and the gridlock at the doors loosened.

The entire scene lasted only minutes but felt like a lifetime.

Behind me, EMTs arrived to tend to Moeda. They staunched her bleeding and transferred her to a board that would slip onto a gurney outside the studio. Within minutes, Moeda was in an ambulance rushing to the hospital, a frantic Ayla by her side.

"Are you okay?" a cop asked.

"Fine. I'm not hurt."

I was mesmerized by the blood on the stage and across my cream-colored Armani.

My suit was ruined.

The police defused the panic and began to question as many people as possible. It was like living in an old *Law & Order* rerun except there was no quick-talking, dour Lenny Briscoe to ease the shock. Sage clung to my side. Although pale and clearly shaken, she wouldn't abandon her beloved aunt.

I told the truth. My staff told the truth. The audience told the truth.

They were all different.

9

John Steen, The NYPD Detective assigned to the case, approached and introduced himself.

"What happened?" I asked.

"I think that's my question," he said gruffly.

"Please," I begged. "I can't . . . don't . . ." I lowered my eyes, unable to find the words.

His face softened. "Of course."

"Tell me," I whispered "I need to know."

The news was grim.

Moeda was unconscious, with a gunshot wound to her head. Ayla was on the way to the hospital with her mother. Mack disappeared. Sage stood by my side.

"How did he do it?" I asked Steen. "How the hell did he get a gun past security?"

Steen was a powerful, 50 something-year old man with broad shoulders and heavily-muscled arms and legs. He wore a somewhat rumpled suit with pants held up by a thick leather belt. He *looked* strong. I imagined that no one dared threaten him. His arms were covered with thick dark hair that poked out from beneath his white dress shirt. Although he had a short, bushy moustache that made him look fierce, he *felt* safe. His clear blue eyes easily shifted from icy to hot to gentle. Icy when he asked about Mack; hot when he questioned Sage; and gentle when he spoke to me.

"He had a *Liberator*," Steen explained. He paused, quiet and respectful.

"A Liberator?"

"Yeah. We found it on the floor. It's a plastic homemade gun. You download the instructions from the Internet and print it out on a 3D machine, free and clear. It shoots a standard bullet and is completely undetectable by the X-Ray scanner machine at the door."

"What about the bullet?"

"The guy told them he had a pacemaker and couldn't go through the scanner. He even had a forged Pacemaker ID card. They patted him down. He hid the bullet beneath his shirt and told them that he bought the white plastic gun on the street – a toy for his grandson."

"Didn't they suspect?"

"Who would suspect a white-haired man who says he has a pacemaker and a gift for his grandson? Remember, these are young security guards."

I shook my head. Baby boomers were just as capable of murder as anyone else. Perhaps now people would realize that they shouldn't be ignored – for better or worse.

"He brought it into the studio," Steen continued. "When Moeda called him disgusting he stood up and shot. The Liberator can only hold one bullet. The guy had good aim."

"He was the leader of a biker gang."

"Makes sense. He hit his target, dropped the plastic gun, and ran. He's lucky, though. The Liberator can hurt the shooter as well as the target. It's not very sophisticated."

I shivered, thinking of Mack as lucky.

"I remember seeing him in the audience. He stood up, angry. No one noticed – their eyes were on the stage. I had no idea what he was going to do until I heard the shot and saw the blood on Moeda . . ."

I choked on my words. Sage put her arm around me.

"We'll find him," Steen said matter-of-factly. "How far can an old man go?"

As far as he wants.

"Did anyone else get hurt?"

"A few bruises and scratches. There weren't enough people in the audience for a real stampede."

Images of stampedes filled my mind.

Cambodia, 2010 – 378 people dead after a festival on a small island.
Egypt, 2012 – 74 soccer fans killed when fans rushed the field
India, 2013 – 36 people killed after a Hindu religious festival
New York: Audience members killed after shots on Truth With Dr. H!

Steen read my mind. "No one was hurt, Doc, except for Moeda."

I nodded.

"The press got wind of this and . . ."

He didn't have to say more. This type of event destroyed shows. A few years ago, John Schmitz was invited to the Jenny Jones tabloid talk show. It was scripted as "a secret admirer who will step forward on national TV" and titled *Same Sex Secret Crushes.* John Schmitz was never told. He convinced himself that his secret admirer was his ex-fiancé. Once on the show, he was confronted with Scott Amedure, a gay man.

John was humiliated, convinced everyone thought he was gay. He went home and a few days later, shot and killed Scott Amedure in cold blood.

Critics called it a "dirty ambush." The show never aired. Producers admitted they lied to Schmitz in order to get him to come onstage. Schmitz was sentenced to life in jail. The show was sued for $25 million and eventually cancelled.

Would that be the fate of *Truth With Dr. H?*

Were we as guilty as Jenny Jones?

"The bullet," Steen continued, intrigued with the details, "caused some bleeding. The entry wound was small; the exit wound large."

"That's where the blood . . ." I looked down at my Armani suit, "came from."

"Yes. It wasn't deep in the brain but these wounds are very unpredictable. No one can accurately foresee the outcome."

I shrugged.

Nothing to say. Poor Moeda – but did I really care?

"Let's go home," Sage said.

"The back door," Steen suggested. "Follow me and I'll show you out."

"Thank you."

He touched my arm. I shivered. Sage led me backstage and I changed into spare trousers and a loose-fitting shirt. I threw my Armani suit into the trash bin. We followed Steen through the bowels of the building, emerging on the street. He hailed a cab and we headed downtown.

"Munsee Court," Steen said to the driver.

I wondered how The Detective knew my address.

Steen stood at the curb, watching us as we were sucked into the heavy midtown traffic.

I was going home.

Where I thought it was safe.

10

The cab brought us to South William Street.

I loved my block. History lived here like a friendly neighbor, gently but consistently asserting its presence. The city's best kept secret was that the soul of New York was born in New Amsterdam and not London.

Here on this street I was connected to my Dutch legacy. I felt their 500 year old presence as if they still walked the streets and sailed the waters in elegant brigantines.

Now South William was in the heart of the financial district, one of busiest areas of the city. During the week it was crowded with workers, businesspeople, and tourists. *Gucci*-clad power brokers shared narrow streets with grease-stained laborers, illegals, wide-eyed spectators, and an occasional mother pushing an $1800 *Bugaboo* stroller. *Prada* rushed alongside *Walmart* specials; $1000 *Jimmy Choo* shoes shared the pavement with battered sneakers. Every language, race, and ethnicity was represented, along with some of the most powerful financiers in the world. The constant music of construction paired with taxis, cars, limos, and trucks created a cacophony that echoed Neil Diamond's *Beautiful Noise*.

The financial soul of the area was represented by Arturo Di Modica's charging bronze bull. It was originally "dropped" on Broad Street in front of the Stock Exchange, after the 1987 market crash. The16-foot long, 7100-pound creature was later installed in Bowling Green by popular demand. The bull became an icon for fierce financial aggression – head lowered, tail curled, poised for attack. It was strange that a world-renown icon was only a few minutes from my home, confronting a daily blur of tourists.

Alongside the bull, spirits of Peter Stuyvesant and the Munsee Indians wandered the streets in names, twisted lanes, and carefully placed plaques to recall their heydays. Periodically, I would follow the markers in the middle of Wall Street, placed there to memorialize the outline of the original 17th century Dutch Wall.

South William Street, running parallel to Stone Street, was one of the oldest streets in the city. Included in the official Stone Street Historic District, its original name was *Slyck Straet* or Muddy Lane. In 1654, when the Sephardic Jews arrived from Recife, it became known as Jew's Alley.

I stared up at buildings that obliterated the sky and thought about the original Dutch structures lost in the Great Fire of 1835. My home, *Munsee Court,* was built in 1927, named for the Lenape Indians who traded Manhattan to Peter Minuit in 1626. Eight years ago it was converted into upscale condos. I bought a three-bedroom unit – one of 30 in the building. It came with a private elevator, water view, and a spacious outdoor terrace. It cost me every penny I had.

My neighbors were arrogant giants like One Wall Trade Center and The Goldman Sachs Building, skinned in limestone and situated on the "most expensive real estate in New York." Nearby, 40 Wall Street was once the tallest structure in the world until the Empire State Building was completed in 1931. Originally the Bank of Manhattan building, it had the dubious honor of being the site of an accidental plane crash in 1946. A U.S. Army Airforce C-45 Beechcraft slammed into the north side at the 58th floor, creating a 20x10 foot hole.

Years later, a new owner purchased 40 Wall Street, put his name on the building, and in 1998 it was designated as a New York City Landmark.

Welcome to the neighborhood, *The* Donald.

Across the street was my favorite "storefront" – Tiffany & Co. It caught my eye every time I passed.

Sage was not concerned with our elegant neighbors. She decided to move in with me because she believed that my condo was too big for a single, aging professional and her Maine Coon cat, Mirasol. Together, the three of us made a dramatic transition from basic shelter to feline aristocracy. I believed that we *all* loved it. My condo was home.

"You love it here," Sage said softly.

"Yes."

We paused to admire the entrance to my building.

I spoke slowly and deliberately. "This place gives me a sense of . . . connection, as if I lived here before, long ago in another life."

Sage didn't get it. She changed the subject, bringing us back to the moment. "You pay too much attention to your audiences."

"I'm still in shock. How did that happen on *my* show?"

She shrugged. "You never know what people will do. If I learned anything in school, it's to expect the unexpected."

"I do . . . but this?" Images of the stampeding audience and bloodied Moeda filled my head. I should have known, by this time in my life, that psychopaths stalked my family.

"You're Dr. H – *everyone* knows you."

"For better or worse." I paused. "Do you know," I said, admiring my building, "that in 1660 there was a psychopath who roamed New Amsterdam, preying on Jews who lived on this very street?"

Sage shuddered. "I didn't know but it doesn't matter. That was 500 years ago."

"Our ancestors were there."

Sage touched the hamsa on her neck. "We have a lot of ancestors. I prefer to think about the Indian and the red-headed slave girl."

I laughed. "Always the romantic."

"Who really cares about New Amsterdam?"

"You should. It's in your blood."

"Karma? Gilgul? All that stuff?"

"No. Haunted family trees with twisted psychopaths."

It was only an instant but I saw it in Sage's eyes – a brief flash of memory. The same that simmered inside me, as if we held a secret tucked safely in our collective unconscious.

"Let's go upstairs," Sage said quickly.

We headed for the private elevator and rose eight stories to a space that was the latest point in our haunted family tree. From 15th century Spain and Portugal, 17th century New Amsterdam, to the present day, we were like glittering raindrops – trapped in the tangled branches of psychopaths and their prey.

11

Tamirah was waiting for us in the foyer. She had let herself in with the key I gave her when I moved into the condo.

"Are you okay? Do you need a body guard?" She demanded, flipping the luscious brown hair that rested on her shoulders.

I stared at her. "How do you know . .?"

"I *always* know. I'm your business manager and it's my job to know everything."

Tamirah tightened her lips and narrowed her eyes. She was right – somehow, Tamirah always *knew*.

We had been friends since the days, so long ago, when we lived across the street from each other in newly-developed Levittown, Long Island. My sister Espie and Mother found it hard to make friends in the brand new vanilla community. Their strange "look" – red hair, hazel eyes, and dark skin stood out among the white, unremarkable faces that peopled our street. Espie and Mother seemed part Sephardic and something else – an undefinable mix that probably belonged to a long lost family secret.

Father and I were different. Father loved it and was proud of owning his new, cookie-cutter home. Tamirah and I became best friends. We were the only Jews on the block *and* the same age; we liked the same flavor ice cream; and whispered similar secrets. We were comfortable in the blandness of suburban life, never fully blending into the frenzy of our previous city neighborhoods. We didn't miss sitting on stoops, playing punch ball, and darting around pickle carts. Levittown was clean, simple, and quiet.

We shared our most precious secrets, including our crushes on the boy next door. Tamirah called him "Dutchboy" and the name stuck. I jealously watched Tamirah and her secret rendezvous with Dutchboy. They sneaked into his bedroom and "did things" that Tamirah refused to reveal. Perhaps I really didn't want to *know*?

The only thing that Tamirah talked about was his small box of ivory dominoes. She was not allowed to touch it. Once, she took a domino out of the box and Dutchboy went wild, throwing her out of his room. Tamirah never did *that* again.

Later, when Dutchboy grew up and became The Senator, Tamirah would see him privately in his office. It was during one of those visits that she secured FRS sponsorship for *Truth With Dr. H!* Without Tamirah, there may not have been a show at all. I made Tamirah my business manager and shared everything, including The *Perfect* Idea.

Sage glared at Tamirah. "Hanya is tired. She doesn't need to think about money now."

Sage disliked my exquisitely pragmatic friend who thought in numbers the same way most of us thought in pictures.

"She always needs to think about money," Tamirah preached. "A little girl like you should know better."

Sage's eyes flashed. She was poised to come back with an equal insult when I intervened. I had no patience for bickering.

"You're right Tamirah. And you're right Sage. Now is not the time."

Tamirah was feisty, a genius at numbers, business, and organization. She was much less acclimated to people.

"Now," I continued before either of them could stop me, "I have to rest and integrate everything that happened."

Tamirah jingled the key to my apartment that she carried on a small gold metal *Dr. H!* key ring. She scowled. "Don't wait too long."

"I promise. Tomorrow we'll talk."

She glanced at Sage.

"Tomorrow," she said stiffly and pushed the button for the elevator. "But no later than that."

"I promise."

Sage nodded as Tamirah entered the elevator, and we crossed the foyer, heading into the cocoon I called home. We paused at the custom-made country kitchen table carved from *acacia* wood. In the Bible, God ordered The Israelites to make a box of acacia wood to hold the stone tablets containing the Ten Commandments – known as the Ark of the Covenant.

My table felt like a subtle connection to my ancient origins. It was a magnificent, handmade piece. To please Sage, I had placed a crystal dish filled with truffles from *Chocolate Works*. Each truffle was hand crafted and decorated.

Sage's connection to chocolate was just as spiritual as mine was to acacia wood.

Sage stared at the plate. "The best," she said softly, carefully selecting a dark chocolate caramel and putting it on her tongue.

I sighed. I didn't like chocolate. Thankfully, *Chocolate Works* made several truffles that I enjoyed. I choose the red velvet, pretending to share Sage's passion. Sage watched me trying to mimic her.

She shook her head and smiled sadly.

12

Tamirah arrived early the next morning. She carried the large, chestnut-colored *Tumi Beacon Hill* leather laptop briefcase that I had given her for her 65th birthday. It was a beautiful piece.

"Good morning," Tamirah said stiffly. "Are you ready to talk?"

"Why don't you join us?" I smiled.

"You know that I only drink coffee."

"Figures," Sage mumbled.

I led her to the country kitchen table where Sage and I had been drinking tea and eating cronuts from Ansel's bakery in Soho. Tamirah stared at the cronuts.

"I see you're eating Dominique's specialty." Tamirah frowned. She didn't personally *know* Dominique Ansel, the infamous baker known for his cronuts – a creative cross between croissants and donuts.

Tamirah sat at the table, placing her briefcase next to her.

"We have to talk, Hanya. Things like this can have an impact on earnings . . ."

Tamirah was interrupted by a call from the doorman. Sage got up, crossed the room, and pressed the speaker button as Tamirah continued. "It can be good or bad. We have to make it *good* to protect your assets."

"I . . ."

Remez's voice interrupted. "A woman named Ayla is looking for you."

"Ayla?" Tamirah said. "Isn't that the woman who was your guest yesterday? Her mother was shot . . .?"

Sage and I looked at one another.

"Yes."

"Is she safe? Good for business?"

No one spoke.

"I don't think you should let her in," Tamirah concluded.

"How can we not? What would the press say if we refused?"

Sage waited.

"How can we not?" I repeated thoughtfully.

"I don't like it," Sage said softly.

"I don't either – but we have no choice. Her mother was *shot* on my show."

Tamirah shrugged. "It can go wrong very quickly."

I didn't like her inference. Potential headlines flashed through my mind.

TV shrink meets with daughter of woman shot on show. Are they working together?

The opposite was equally offensive.

TV shrink rejects distraught daughter of attempted murder victim.

"It's a Catch-22?" I mumbled.

"Of course."

"I don't understand," Sage frowned. She hated when I used old references.

"Damned if you do . . . damned if you don't."

Sage shook her head and spoke into the speaker.

"Is she alone, Remez?"

"Yes."

"Does she look . . . dangerous?"

"No. A little . . ." he paused.

"Disheveled?" Sage filled in the word. "She's the daughter of the woman shot on *Truth With Dr. H!*"

"I know."

Sage looked at me with a question in her eyes.

"Send her up," I frowned.

"Are you sure?"

"I'm sure."

How could I have known that my consent would plunge us deeper into psychopathic crosshairs? Like the ancient wolves and humans, we never lived far apart.

13

Ayla looked and smelled awful. She stood in my foyer like an overflowing trash can on Park Avenue.

"I haven't left my mother's side since she was shot," Ayla explained.

"Dr. H has had a tough time as well," Tamirah said, hugging her briefcase protectively.

Ayla stared at her blankly.

"I just want you to know that," Tamirah added.

"Who the hell are you?" Ayla snapped.

"I'm the doctor's business manager. I look out for her best interests."

"Sure," Ayla scowled. "I'm not looking out for *any* interests. My mother might be dying as we speak. The world has eye-witnessed murder. Nothing is more important."

"The show was taped," Tamirah retorted.

There was an awkward silence.

"You need a shower," I said gently. "Tamirah, you should go back to your office. I'll be in touch."

Tamirah scowled.

I took Ayla's elbow and turned her away from Tamirah. "Let's go, dear."

I led her down the hall. Sage hid behind her cronuts and tea. Their eyes followed me but I refused to be drawn into their suspicions. Tamirah and Sage didn't like poor people. They were far more comfortable with the wealthy, anxious, and depressed denizens of the Upper East Side.

Ayla and I went through the living room and into the guest bathroom. It was an elegant bathroom – marble veined countertops, mirrors, and a sleek glass vessel sink. Ayla's eyes widened. I wondered if Ayla had ever seen such luxury.

I handed her a soft Turkish towel, and pointed to expensive soaps and lotions displayed on a shelf. "We'll talk when you're finished. Use the bathrobe on the hook."

I closed the door and returned to the country kitchen table.

"Do you think that's wise?" Sage asked.

I shrugged. "What other choice?"

"Get her a hotel."

"Too late for that. The woman just saw her mother shot on national TV. She doesn't need to be thrust into a cold, sterile hotel room."

"It was taped," Tamirah said again.

I also saw doubt in Sage's eyes. Tamirah clutched her briefcase like an AK-47.

"I have no choice." I poured a second cup of tea and sat.

"I think . . ." Sage began, but the phone rang. It was Griet Vansalee, my executive producer. I put it on speaker so they could hear.

"How are we doing?" I asked.

Griet sighed. "Moeda is still in the hospital. Non-responsive."

"Terrible."

"I heard Ayla is staying with you."

"News travels fast. She's taking a shower now. After that . . ."

"Ayla *is* staying with you," Griet said stiffly. "Do you understand?"

"I thought . . ."

"I don't care what you thought. The woman is staying in your condo with you."

I was silent. Apparently, there was no room for argument.

"We made a decision," Griet continued. "*Truth With Dr. H!* is going on temporary hiatus. The police haven't found Mack and believe it's dangerous to continue taping. He might be stalking any one of us."

I nodded, although Griet couldn't see the fear in my eyes. Sage sighed, a mixture of relief and anger. Tamirah frowned. "I understand," I said stiffly.

"Of course you understand."

"It's my job," I said so softly that I wasn't sure the executive producer heard.

"We would like you to come down to the studio and tape a short message. Something about our prayers for Moeda and the ongoing search for the perpetrator."

"Of course."

"Our lawyers say it's essential."

Sage shook her head and was about to say something. I raised my index finger against my lips.

Not a word.

"I understand completely, Griet. We have to do what's good for the show."

Griet hesitated, as if considering her next words. "It's about ratings," she said flatly. "We don't want to lose our ratings. We want everyone to think . . . know . . . that we're a compassionate operation and the well-being of our guests comes first."

"You told me our ratings were great."

"I lied," Griet frowned.

"You lied?"

"I didn't want to trouble you. Our ratings have been dropping for quite a while."

I was shocked.

"With all this going on," Griet continued, "I want our viewers to see us as kind . . . nurturing. Come up this afternoon for the taping."

There was no other response. "I'll be there."

"Fine. One more thing."

"Yes?"

"The FRS Clinic is sending over an investigative videographer to follow the story."

"What story?"

"*This one.* About Ayla and Moeda. The *positive* intent behind the show. The staff. And the investigation to find the perpetrator."

"I don't think . . ."

"It doesn't matter what you or I think. FRS is our biggest sponsor. They also read the ratings. If we want to keep them, we do what they say. They must be happy."

Anger rose in the back of my throat.

"The investigative videographer's name is Robert," Griet added quickly.

"*Who* is Robert?"

"You have to understand, Hanya. These things are political. I do what they say, not what you or I want."

"*Who* is Robert?" I repeated.

Griet sighed, louder this time. "The Senator's Son. The Senator who *founded* FRS."

FRS – *Family Reigns Supreme* – was The Senator's creation. It grew with the man so now, nearly forty years later; it was a major New York foundation and mental health facility that gleefully accepted Medicare, Medicaid, and all private insurers.

Sage waved her arms furiously.

"Of course," I said bitterly. "I'll leave Sage with Ayla, tape the message, and meet your Robert."

"I knew I could count on you."

Griet clicked off the speaker before I could say goodbye.

"How can you?" Sage demanded, her hazel eyes filled with fire.

"How can I *not*?"

"You have no choice," Tamirah said smugly. "It's in the contract."

14

I wore my forest green *Versace* suit with an ivory tank and a loosely tied *Hermes* silk scarf. I wouldn't allow Sage to come with me. Tamirah left for her midtown office and Sage disappeared into the electronic pages of a psychology text. Ayla stared at the screen, mesmerized by daytime TV.

I left my building and Remez hailed a cab for me. By the time I got through the studio beneath the curious eyes of the building security, Griet was waiting for me with her "shadow," studio attorney, Jake Visch Esq. Visch was a well-known foodie – every tie he wore had a stain. His yellow tie had tiny specks of red chili sauce. Griet never said hello. Instead, she frowned, and handed me a script. I read it quickly.

I never liked Griet. She was a compulsive woman who improved her looks with expensive clothes and costly appointments with famous Manhattan stylists. Her brown eyes were flat, her thin lips permanently molded into a frown, and her cheekbones jutted like elbows beneath thin, aging skin.

I followed Griet into the studio. She studied me as I read the statement carefully. Griet watched it flash on the screen, nodding with approval. It would appear to our TV audience. The naked truth.

I hated the words.

Thank you for your loyalty. We have been advised to temporarily suspend the show.
Please tune in at our regular time to watch past episodes.

Mack, the shooter, is still at large. The NYPD is conducting a full scale investigation to apprehend him. If you have any information about Mack, the baby, or the investigation, please leave a message on our website, call the studio, or contact the police. The NYPD Officer in charge of the case is Detective John Steen.

We're offering a $10,000 reward for information that leads to Mack's capture.

God Bless You.
Hold on to your truths! Pray with us for the speedy recovery of Moeda and her missing grandson.

Griet nodded when I finished. "Good job."

"You wrote it."

"Not really. The lawyers wrote it – I just edited."

"Only $10,000 reward?"

"The recommended amount. Too much will lead to fake reports. Make it harder to find Mack."

"Harder for whom?"

Griet sighed. She nodded and a man stepped forward. He was tall and thin, mid-forties, with a plastic smile on his face. His eyes were glazed; his hair caramel-colored and expertly styled to look tousled even when sprayed to stay in place.

"This is Robert," Griet smiled obsequiously.

Robert held out his hand.

"The Senator's Son?" I took his hand. It was dry and cool.

"Yes, Doctor, I'm The Senator's Son but I can assure you that I got this job because I was the best man. Once you see me work, you'll understand." He gazed at me with cool blue eyes.

"I hope so."

He tilted his head in a charming, boyish gesture. "Give me the chance, ma'am, and ya'll be very pleased," he said in a fake southern accent.

"We'll see."

Griet glared at me.

"And this," Robert returned to his New York private school voice. He yanked a tiny, blonde girl dressed in pink, in front of him. She looked no more than 14 years old, "is Isobel . . . my assistant."

"You're his assistant?"

"I look younger than I am," she reassured me in a small, high-pitched voice. "I'm highly trained with a lot of experience."

"Of course." I offered my hand.

Isobel's grip was weak and damp.

"She was hired personally by my father," Robert added.

"The Senator?"

"Yes."

A tiny smile flickered on Isobel's lips. She tossed her head defiantly and glanced tenderly at Robert.

"Of course. Where do we begin?"

"I've already done the preliminary work," Robert smiled cavalierly.

"You work fast."

"Yes. And hard."

"So if you've already done the preliminary work, what's the next step?"

"I want to interview you and Ayla in your condo."

I glanced at Griet, who narrowed her eyes.

I had no choice.

"Of course. Let me go home and talk to Ayla and my niece, Sage."

"Sage?"

"Yes. She's my intern and lives with me."

Robert slowly ran the tip of his tongue along his lower lip.

"I understand," he said seductively, "that Ayla is living with you."

"She is now," Griet said quickly. The woman shook her head slightly. Obviously, she wasn't quite as slick as the investigative videographer.

"Yes . . . I guess she is."

Robert reached out and touched my arm suggestively.

You're 20 years younger than me, asshole.

I pulled away.

"Let's set up a time for tomorrow."

Robert, in a rare moment, consented.

15

Robert arrived the next day with Isobel in tow. She wore a tiny pink tee and lugged the camera on her shoulder. They stepped from the elevator and he scanned my apartment, quickly estimating its value. I could see the dollar signs in his eyes.

He held out a box of *La Maison Du Chocolat.*

"Chocolate," Robert said in his velvet voice, "for the admirable doctor."

I took the chocolate and tossed it on the small table in the foyer. "This is Sage," I introduced my niece, purposely not thanking him.

Sage was dressed in jeans and a snug-fitting red shirt. A spark of interest flashed in her eyes and was quickly covered up.

"You're Dr. H's niece?" Robert said glibly, dressed in dark jeans and an Anderson Cooper style button-down shirt. He played the part well.

"Yes. I'm her intern. I'm also a doctoral student."

"In what?"

"Psychology."

Robert nodded as if she had identified herself as the President's daughter, and offered his hand. Sage took it soberly.

Isobel watched, frowning. I wondered how many times she had observed this scene with her boss.

"And this," I pulled Ayla from behind us, "is Ayla."

Ayla was dressed in the studio clothes she wore on the day of the shooting. Although she was clean and hair neatly pulled into a barrette, she looked tired, her eyes dull.

Robert didn't offer his hand. "How is Moeda?"

Ayla shrugged.

"No change," I interjected.

"I'm very sorry," Robert said, using the socially appropriate body language.

There was a brief, tense silence.

"I would like to interview . . . all of you," Robert smiled demurely. He overplayed the part. No one seemed to notice but me. Was it my age that prevented me from being affected by his plastic good looks and charm? I shrugged off the thought and glanced at Isobel. She was peering down the hallway, trying to get a glimpse of what lay beyond. She carried the huge camera on her shoulder and a bag of heavy equipment. The Senator's Son wasn't refined enough to help the tiny young woman with her burden.

"Where would you like to shoot? We can do it in my living room or on the terrace, which is quite large."

Robert's eyes met mine. His face hardened.

He knows my dance. Be careful.

"I imagine," he said curtly, "that the Great Room would be more conducive."

The Great Room. He had checked out the building and read the floor plans online. Only realtors called it the "great room."

"Of course."

I led them down the hall, past the country kitchen table and into the 41 foot room, complete with two glossy Italian marble fireplaces. Isobel paused, her mouth slightly open. The room was painted in a soft blue-grey with a cream-colored custom leather sofa and Brazilian wood entertainment center on the near end. A nine-piece *Courtrai*-style dining set with a golden flax finish, matching breakfront and chairs, completed the open-plan dining area. Floor-to-ceiling windows graced the outside walls, with French doors leading to the 50 foot terrace. A combination of abstract paintings and black & white photographs were displayed artfully on the wall. Motorized shades were mounted on each window to parade or cancel the magnificent views of lower New York.

Robert was not impressed. He pointed to the couch. "Please sit." He pulled a dining room chair close to us and began his questions, using a soft, cajoling screen voice.

I caught my breath at the sound of his voice. He spoke smoothly with a sensual undertone in all his words. I tried to defend myself against his lure – a fish caught in a widening net. Nothing felt sincere about him but what did I know? I was still numb from the bizarre turn of events. Could I have predicted this as well?

I glanced at Isobel – the pretty little girl in pink. She obediently shot the footage.

Mirasol jumped into my lap. She curled up in a mass of soft fur. Robert leaned over to pet her.

The cat hissed.

Sage

1

No way would I let a box of *La Maison Du Chocolat* languish untouched on a table in the foyer. I grabbed it and brought the box into the living room with the rest of us.

I confess – I liked Robert immediately. Maybe it was the Anderson Cooper shirt or the easy way he wore his jeans. Perhaps it was his smooth broadcast voice that barely escaped being monotone. I wondered if his smile, plastic but studied, was the feature that ultimately snared me. I'm not sure.

I wanted The Senator's Son and knew that Hanya wouldn't approve. Perhaps that made him more appealing? Add that with his celebrity and the man was intoxicating.

Hanya and I shared history as well as living space. She knew me better than my own mother, who was more interested in clothes than people. Hanya was a substitute for my beloved Grandma Espie who died tragically years ago. No one understood me better than Grandma Espie. Hanya took me in and became my role model in psychology. Ironically, Hanya needed me as much as I needed her. We made a solid team. At the same time, Hanya was also my harshest critic.

She rarely liked my friends and never liked my boyfriends. Hanya loved my studies and my ideas, feeding off changes in the field like a media shark hungering for leads. I forgave her for aggressive demands that I reveal *everything*.

It was in her blood.

I kept secrets, knowing Hanya wouldn't approve. She convinced herself that I was completely open – a bottomless trough of data.

I evolved into a skilled white liar, dusting truth with distraction, and eliminating critical bits of information. I wasn't completely successful but Hanya played ignorant as if granting me sanctuary from her scrutiny. It worked for both of us.

Hanya loved me and tried hard to replace my loss when her sister died, but never quite succeeded. Esperanza – Grandma Espie – was a warm, timeless soul finding her way through a superficial world. Hanya was the opposite – cool and controlled. She never married, never had children, and as far as I knew, never had any serious relationships. I suspected that Hanya saw sex as loss of control, like walking on thin ice. She never understood why I craved intimacy, spurned unimaginative missionary sex, and loved kinky erotica. Men were my passion. Sweaty, hungry sex was almost as good as chocolate.

Perhaps it came from my first love, my cousin Joshua, who could talk me in or out of anything?

Joshua. I tried not to think about him but he lingered in my head, ready to pounce. Joshua never led to a good place. I constantly forced myself to shift to another man - and another - endlessly negotiating lovers. Joshua and I never made love but shared a childhood seduction that was forever embedded in my soul. There were many men after Joshua but none replaced my cousin. I counted them like notches on my belt; they came and left, usually by my choice.

I checked Robert's hand. No wedding band. Robert would be my next notch; it was inevitable. I was immediately smitten when The Senator's Son arrived at our apartment. I have that habit with men – falling quickly and recovering slowly. Add to it gourmet chocolate and I was easily, and willingly, lured into pleasure.

.

Robert was somewhat different than his predecessors. He didn't arrive with *just* chocolate – his offering was *La Maison Du Chocolat*. Hanya took the chocolate, packed in a rich brown box with ribbon, and tossed it on the table in the foyer. I saw immediately that Robert had selected a collection of hand-made *timeless ganaches*. I couldn't stop thinking about the offering – *Caracas, Guayaquil* and others that electrified the taste buds. Only the most refined men even knew about *La Maison*.

Hanya was unimpressed. For a brief moment, she was suspicious. I lowered my eyes and frowned so she believed I was on her side, barely noticing the chocolate. It could have been a title for a new show.

Women who use men for chocolate and sex.

I suppressed a laugh. I had to be sensitive – Hanya wasn't at her best. Her show was temporarily suspended, a woman was fighting for her life because an old guy took a shot with a one-bullet homemade gun, and a strange-looking woman moved in at the executive producer's order. It was bizarre; a comedy of postmodern errors. Hanya was at a loss – a condition in which she rarely found herself. The woman needed to be in control; any slip of the leash and she began to crumble into the frail, least-favored daughter of her childhood. I had to handle her carefully.

I still longed for Grandma Espie. She would have loved Robert's lineage and his chocolate. Grandma had a sense of adventure, a love for the strange and exotic. After her violent death years ago, I changed my name. No one knew that I was now legally Sage Esperanza. Along with the hamsa, it was another way to always have Espie with me.

Hanya interrupted my thoughts as she introduced me to Robert. "This is Sage."

"You're Dr. H's niece?" Robert said glibly. He shook my hand and electricity raced up my arm like a heroine in a trash romance novel. I stared at his silky, caramel-colored hair and unflinching blue eyes. There was no turning back. Sure, I knew he was more than twenty years older than me. Who cared? After all, Ayla's Mack was even older. Of course, Mack wasn't the best example of successful relationships but any man who brought *La Maison Du Chocolat* as an introduction had to be great in bed.

Hanya led us to the living room. Isobel, Robert's assistant, followed obediently. Robert pointed to the couch and we all sat as Isobel set up the camera. I placed the chocolate on the side table next to me.

I glanced at Ayla. She was an odd woman, with stringy, caramel-colored hair and blue eyes, similar in color to Robert. Yet they were worlds apart. Robert's charisma was clearly broadcasted while Ayla's sad, sour face always seemed somewhere else. There was a distant look in her eyes. Was she worried about Moeda? Thinking about Mack? Praying that she would find the baby she abandoned? She was an unfinished puzzle that I tried to read, but failed.

The cat, Mirasol, jumped into Hanya's lap. Robert tried to pet her but Mirasol hissed.

Robert flashed a beguiling smile. "The pussy doesn't like people," he growled.

Hanya glared at him.

Robert quickly edited his tone. "Let's begin the interview."

I wondered if Robert was like his father, The Senator? There had been so many rumors and accusations through the years. The Senator's storied career was stained with whispers of him preferring too-young women, endless affairs, and unclaimed children . . . many media people had tried to prove that much of The Senator's wealth went to paying off his indiscretions. No one could ever substantiate it. Bloggers claimed that The Senator was so powerful he could corrupt DNA reports and dead-end paper trails. The Senator always emerged stronger after these accusations, with his now-famous words, "thank you, thank you, thank you."

Everyone loved The Senator.

"Fine," I smiled at Robert, "let's begin."

Hanya glared at me and turned to Robert. "Ask your questions," she ordered.

Robert smirked.

2

Ayla was describing how she ran away with Mack when the doorman buzzed.

"I'll get it," I said quickly.

Hanya looked at me gratefully.

I went into the foyer and pressed the speaker that connected with Remez.

"A small priority envelope," the doorman said quickly, "for Ayla – marked "Confidential" and "Do Not X-Ray.""

"Who sent it?"

"No return. A messenger on a bicycle dropped it off."

I hesitated. There were so many snail mail dangers like letter bombs and poisons, you had to be cautious.

"It's light – nothing heavy inside," Remez added.

It was probably get well cards. Why would anyone want to hurt Ayla? Mack shot Moeda, not his ex.

"Does it look safe?"

"I don't see anything out of the ordinary," the doorman replied. "Of course you can't always tell by looking at it."

I made the decision that would later haunt me. "Let's take the chance. It sounds okay. Send it up."

Remez delivered the small manila envelope in minutes. I brought it into the living room where Ayla was describing Mack's tattoos – a Nazi Iron Eagle on his chest and SS lightning bolts on his thigh, pointing to his penis. Robert was listening carefully, his eyebrows raised slightly in mock surprise.

"This is for you." I handed the envelope to Ayla and sat back on the couch.

Robert and Hanya looked at me, then Ayla. Isobel continued shooting.

"Who knows I'm here?" Ayla asked, pushing a wisp of hair from her face.

I shrugged.

Who cares?

Ayla knew I didn't trust her. Maybe the weary woman had once been pretty? Maybe there was sweetness beneath the years of hard living? Bikers, sex, drugs, and booze were all part of her resume. She looked ten years older than her age, her skin creased where all-too-soon there would be deep wrinkles, and her hair was hopelessly listless. Her eyes sagged into blue pools of melancholy.

"I don't know. The doorman said a messenger delivered it."

Ayla turned the envelope over. "Why would anyone send me something here?"

"Do you want to open it?" Robert asked impatiently, "or would you prefer privacy?" He glanced directly into the camera.

Ayla shrugged. "I don't need privacy. What do I have to hide?"

You're already hiding too much.

Hanya scowled. "Why don't we finish the interview and then you can open it?"

Ayla shrugged. "I'll do it now."

It was a strange discussion. We were talking about an envelope. "Open it," I said irritably. "Then we can move on."

Robert looked at me and returned to Ayla.

Good body language.

We watched Ayla as if she was a filler between commercials. She opened the flap and slowly, theatrically, peered inside.

Ayla's eyes widened. She screamed and dropped the envelope. It fell to the floor, spilling a dirty-looking powder on the rug.

3

Anthrax? Ricin?

"No one move," Robert hovered over the powder. Ayla rubbed her hands together like Lady Macbeth washing off blood. Isobel panned the entire scene.

I stood up, trembling. "Don't move," I echoed Robert. "I'll call the police."

"Call Steen," Hanya hissed, slipping a card from her pocket. Part of me wondered why she had The Detective's card so handy. Hanya rarely held on to business cards.

"Done." I rushed for the nearest phone on the end table next to the couch, beside the box of *La Maison Du Chocolat*.

Hanya pulled Ayla and Robert away from the powder. Isobel backed off, continuing to tape. She didn't seem concerned.

My heart raced.

"Out," Robert ordered.

We cowered in the foyer, as far from the powder as possible, waiting for Steen. Isobel reluctantly followed. It felt like hours before Steen and the police arrived. Later, I was told it was only six minutes.

Steen immediately assumed command.

The apartment filled with first responders in white hazmat suits breathing through respirators. Windows were checked, the living room sealed off, and the condo buzzed with activity. Public health workers ordered us to strip off our clothes and handed us special soap. Our clothing was put in sealed, marked bags and placed in a large plastic box. Each box was secured in an isothermal container. Robert stared at my nudity but I was too frightened to care. He was oddly calm.

We slipped into sterile hospital scrubs and were grilled by antiterrorist officers.

Who delivered the envelope?

Who opened the envelope?

Do you have any idea who might have sent it?

Why would they target you?

There was no indication that it was Mack, but no one could be sure of anything.

They herded us around the country kitchen table and sealed off the living room with plastic. We were advised that the powder was being tested and we wouldn't know the results for a few days. They recommended we start on the antibiotic, Ciprofloxacin, in case it turned out positive. We were terrified.

People in hazmat suits surrounded us, becoming a blur of color and motion.

They transported us to a quarantined hospital room with beds, a TV, table, and small couch. We were ordered to remain as they decontaminated the apartment and waited for test results to identify the powder.

Were we going to live or die? I felt suspended in a quivering time warp, hovering between prank and bioterrorist attack. Ayla broke down in tears and Hanya tended to her, using rusty crisis intervention techniques. Robert and I watched silently. Every so often he would stroke my back or shyly hold my hand.

Isobel was allowed to tape everything except our nudity.

"Mack," Ayla cried, her wails reverberating through the quarantine room. "How could you do this?"

They gave us access, through telephone and cell, to the outside world. We avoided calls from the media and news on TV.

Tamirah struggled to hide her delight. "This is *very* good for business."

Hanya was shocked but said nothing. She always forgave Tamirah.

Griet told Hanya that the press was everywhere, asking questions, speculating, wondering how a 73 year old man could wreak such havoc. Photos of Mack appeared on TV, the Internet, and in newspapers. He looked like a kindly old man.

Or maybe a kindly old psychopath?

4

It was talcum powder. Rose-scented, tinted gray.

We were allowed to go home, feeling both angry and embarrassed. Angry because we were victims of a prank; embarrassed for the same reason. There had been so much commotion over talcum powder. The Late Night TV comedians included us in their opening monologues.

Murder by talcum powder.
Will the real scent please rise?
Ricin on the mind.

Even Anderson Cooper mentioned talcum powder on his *RidicuList*. Everyone was laughing but us. An enterprising businessperson made up tee-shirts with pink cans of Dr. H! talcum printed on the front and sold them on the streets. They were sold out by the end of the week.

"It was probably some jaded fan," Hanya said.

No one believed her.

Steen requested an interview as soon as possible. He grudgingly agreed to come to the condo where everyone would be most comfortable, and Robert could tape the scene. Steen didn't like the camera but after a request from The Senator's office, he complied.

No one denied The Senator.

Steen wore a somewhat rumpled suit with what Hanya called the "Peter Sellers" look. I didn't know who Peter Sellers was but Hanya mumbled something about Inspector Clouseau from *The Pink Panther*. I checked him out online and didn't think Hanya's description was very complimentary although there was an odd charm to the eccentric detective and the cartoon pink panther was cute. I said nothing. Who can account for taste?

It was an interesting scenario. Ayla, Hanya, Griet, Visch, and I sat on the couch. Visch's tie was stained with green tea ice cream. Robert watched Isobel and the camera, making sure she had the best angles. Tamirah hovered in the corner, out of camera range but observing everything.

"I want to protect your rights," Tamirah said sternly to Hanya. "You can't leave me out again."

Hanya agreed, only if Tamirah watched and said nothing.

"We don't need another voice in this mess," Hanya mumbled.

We settled into the cream-colored couch as Mirasol curled up in Hanya's lap. She began to purr loudly.

"Can't you keep her quiet?" Robert demanded. "She'll screw up the sound track."

"No," Hanya retorted.

Robert didn't respond.

Steen stood, facing us.

"I hate bullies," Visch commented loudly before Steen could begin. I looked at the expensively dressed little attorney and shrugged.

Robert sat next to me, pressing his leg against mine.

Ayla rounded her shoulders and lowered her head in a classic depressive stance.

It was perfect staging.

The name of an old, vintage 1989 movie popped into my head. *Sex, Lies, and Videotape* was about a man who had a fetish of watching videotapes of women confessing their sexual secrets. I wondered what it would be like to confess my sexual fantasies with Robert watching and listening. I imagined him shutting off the camera, leaping at me, and having wild, rough sex on the floor in front of the couch. I plunged deeper into the fantasy, my heart pumping, my fingers twitching, imagining I was touching him.

Steen cleared his throat.

Robert patted my thigh as if he knew what was dancing in my head. Hanya saw, scowled and Robert grinned at her.

I could feel his skin against mine, his mouth open, biting me . . .

Griet stood up.

"Detective Steen," she said authoritatively.

I returned to the present scene, which was just as bizarre as what was in my head.

Steen cleared his throat again. Clearly, he knew how to handle her. "Please sit down." He took a deep breath and shoved one hand beneath his suit as if clutching a gun. Griet gasped. "I have a few questions," Steen said, his eyes fixed on the executive producer. "And then I'll be out of here."

Griet slunk back into her seat.

"You've all been through quite an ordeal," he continued, "and I'm sure are very tired." He glanced at the camera and noticed the red light. "Do you have to tape this?" Steen knew the answer but had to ask. No one refused The Senator's wishes.

"Move on," Visch grunted.

Steen nodded. "You'll need releases."

Visch sniffed as if Steen's comment didn't deserve a response.

"You've been through an ordeal," Steen repeated. All eyes were on him. Robert's hand moved discreetly up my thigh.

"I have a few questions and then I'll be gone," Steen continued. His eyes shifted to Robert. Again, Robert didn't move. The man wasn't easily scared.

"We were fortunate this time. The envelope was a scare tactic – a prank." Steen sighed. "If we assume that the perpetrator was Mack . . ." Ayla's head shot up. Did I see fire in her eyes? Steen paused and began again. "If we assume that the perpetrator was Mack," he repeated, "then we have to be very careful until he's found. He already tried to kill one person, there's no telling what he would have done if his gun held more than one bullet."

"He would have shot me." Ayla and Hanya spoke at the same time. They looked at one another. Hanya smiled warily.

"He would have shot me," Hanya repeated. "He was angry that I brought Moeda and Ayla to the show. I saw him in the audience . . ."

"You're wrong," Ayla said sharply. "He was after *me*. Angry that I left him, furious that we were talking about *his* baby and how he forced me to abandon it."

Steen waited. We were silent as Ayla forced a few tears down her pale, worn face. "Moeda is still in a coma," she choked, "no one knows if she'll ever come out. He tried to kill her. Now he's going to kill me."

"We have to be careful . . ." Steen's voice was soothing.

"No!" Ayla screamed. "He's a biker. He's head of a biker gang. He has a Nazi Iron Eagle on his chest and has killed many times before . . ."

She jumped up and began pacing around the room, waving her arms frantically. "He wants us all dead. Dead. Do you understand? He won't stop until . . ."

We watched, entertained by her histrionics.

Hanya stood and moved toward the distraught woman. "We'll keep you safe. You'll stay here."

"How? How can I ever feel safe again? Can you bring back Moeda . . ?"

"Moeda will be fine."

"My mother's going to die. I just know it." Ayla fell into Hanya's arms, wailing loudly.

Tamirah moved behind Hanya and patted her client's back. Robert put his arm around my shoulders and pulled me tight against him. Our eyes met briefly.

Steen stood his ground. He waited for Ayla to calm down. "Please, ladies, be seated. And Robert," he lowered his voice, "get your fucking hands off her."

Hanya led Ayla back to the couch as Tamirah backed away. Robert slipped his arm off my shoulder. When everyone settled, Steen sighed audibly and continued.

"You'll be protected. I have officers stationed outside. No one can come in. Every cop in the city is looking for this guy. It shouldn't be hard to find him . . . after all, he's 73 years old. How fast can he move?"

Hanya stiffened. "Are you saying a 73 year old man can't be dangerous?"

"I'm not saying that," Steen responded awkwardly. "Mack's already proven that he's dangerous. It's just that most psychopaths don't live to a ripe old age."

"Ever hear of Bernie Madoff," I retorted. "The Zodiac Killer? Robert Moses? Killaen Van Sickles?"

"Let's not get carried away," Steen interjected. "Not many psychopaths live to an old age unless they're in prison. Even then, they end up getting killed . . ."

"Charles Manson," I ignored him. "Sam Berkowitz, Son of Sam; Dennis Rader, the BTK Killer; Gary Ridgway, The Green River Killer."

"You know a lot about psychopaths," Robert commented.

"Enough!" Hanya ordered. "Let's talk about *our* psychopath."

"Mack." Ayla screamed and started to sob again. Pandemonium broke out – everyone talking and arguing. Robert, realizing that no one was looking, leaned over and licked my neck.

Isobel's camera saw everything.

Suddenly, Steen's cell buzzed. One-by-one all of our cells followed suit. Each of us reached for our phones and then hesitated, realizing we were all receiving texts at the same time. Steen stared at his screen. I looked at mine, along with the others. We all had the same message.

No fear.
I'm going to get all of you.

5

After the interview, when only Hanya, Ayla, and I were left in the condo, Robert texted me.

Meet me @ 7:30

He sent the name and address of an Upper East Side dive bar.

I slipped off the couch, went to the country kitchen table, and grabbed a *Chocolate Works* dark raspberry truffle from the crystal dish. It was like Popeye's spinach – I needed it for strength.

"I'm going out," I said to Hanya, returning to the living room. The creamy sweetness coated my mouth.

"Where? Steen wants us to be careful. You got the same message that we all did."

"To school. The library."

Hanya looked at me quizzically. She started to say something, and then stopped. "Be careful."

"Of course. Stay in crowds, near cops, and take cabs not subways."

Hanya nodded.

"I'll be fine."

I raced into my bedroom, pulled out my best *Victoria's Secret* thong panties and fishnet bra. I changed quickly, slipping jeans and an off-the-shoulder tee on top of the underwear. I sprayed myself with *Chanel Coco Noir* and touched up my makeup.

I waved goodbye to Hanya as I took the elevator down, left Munsee Court, and hailed a cab.

It's going to be a fiery night.

That's what I believed. A few drinks and good sex – exactly what I needed.

I wasn't even close.

6

The bar was crowded, small, and noisy. People pressed up against one another, surveying the drinkers, assessing the market for one-nighters. The lights were dim and the walls covered in an assortment of 60s memorabilia and celebrities. I noticed an old, framed campaign poster of The Senator with hands raised and *Family Reigns Supreme* printed across the bottom. He stood in a day care center surrounded by minority children and their teachers.

"Sage," Robert called. The Senator's Son sat at a tiny round table with one empty chair and two bottles of Microbrew. I pushed my way through the crowd and squeezed in next to him. I hated the city bar scene.

"I hope you like beer." He grinned. "These are the best of the rustic ales – small batch with smoked malts."

I shrugged and tasted the beer. It was good.

Robert nodded with approval.

I wasn't sure what to say. My skin prickled and a drop of sweat ran down between my breasts. "What do you . . . want?"

Robert laughed. "To talk. You can't get in a word with the crew in your aunt's apartment. Especially the damn cat."

I smiled. "No Mirasol or Isobel?"

"Not here."

There was a roar as a local athlete raised his arms in victory on one of the TV screens over the bar.

"You have questions?" I shouted.

Robert touched my cheek, ran his fingers down my neck, and paused just above my breast. He stared steadily into my eyes. "Do I need questions?"

I shrugged off his hand. He laughed.

"I like you Sage."

"It's not the time."

He ran his fingers over my lips. "Sssh. It's always the time. You feel it – I feel it – no need to be coy. We want the same thing."

"Hanya . . ."

"Hanya?" He leaned over and kissed me, forcing his tongue between my lips, exploring my mouth. When he backed away, I was breathless.

"Hanya?" He laughed. "I know what you really want . . ."

"I . . ."

Robert smirked.

"You're 20 years older than me," I objected weakly.

"You're right. That means I know so much more about women than your puny peers who fumble and . . ."

He slipped his hand beneath the table. He squeezed my thigh and ran his fingers against my jeans, between my legs, pressing and rubbing . . . "You like this," he laughed flatly. "Let me show you what an old man can do. Have you ever had an old man?"

"No."

"I thought so."

"I . . ."

"Don't talk."

He rubbed harder, massaging me through the fabric until I couldn't stop him, my breath ragged, the noise and bodies in the bar faded, and I plunged into heart-pounding pressure of his fingers.

I climaxed.

Robert laughed as I caught my breath. "How was that possible?" I gasped.

"Anything is possible. Let me show you."

I was helpless to say no.

He left money on the table and led me out of the crowded, noisy dive bar into the street. I was excited, confused, and drawn to this outlandish, compelling man.

"My place," Robert commanded.

I stared at the strange silhouette created by a bright streetlight. Who *was* this man, and where was I going with him?

7

Robert's apartment was a designer man cave. I could see it on the cover of *Esquire,* in an upscale chick flick, or as the backdrop for a rich man's porn website. The couch was a love seat with grey mohair upholstery, rosewood side panels, and shiny nail heads.

"The couch is called "The Hef" and hand signed by Hugh Hefner," Robert boasted, referring to the aging founder of *Playboy.* "The design commemorated the 50th anniversary of the Playboy

Clubs. It's worth nearly $20,000. He gave it to my father as a gift, who in turn gave it to me." His eyes twinkled.

In front of the loveseat was a black glass coffee table with a small box of old ivory dominoes.

"Don't touch it," Robert barked.

Above the loveseat was a painting – the only wall hanging in the room – with swirls of red, orange, and yellow that looked like an oily abstract of a vagina. The walls were painted in black and gray. Everything was spotlessly clean. No books. No magazines. No ornaments except for a shelf filled with tiny porcelain sculptures.

I crossed the room to examine the sculptures.

"My collection," Robert grinned as he secured the door with a digital door lock, old fashioned sliding chain, and an electronic dead bolt. "You can't be too careful," he sighed, pausing to survey his security.

I touched flesh-colored porcelain of two naked lovers – the faceless female straddled a man's lap as she leaned back almost flat on his knees. The male was upright, his groin against her, his mouth on her breasts. Her hair flowed between his legs as she grasped his calves.

"It's called *Kama Sutra*," Robert said smoothly. "There are so many sex positions that people don't know about. *The Kama Sutra* is an ancient book . . ."

"I know what *The Kama Sutra* is."

"Have you ever tried the positions?"

With my boring lovers?

"Of course."

Robert nodded, not smiling. "Then you're experienced."

"Yes," I lied.

He navigated the space between the door, the shelf, and me. He pulled me into his arms and began to knead his groin against me. I closed my eyes.

Suddenly he pulled away.

I reached for him, but he backed away.

"You want me." He said flatly.

I groaned.

"Say it, bitch. You want me."

I moved toward him and he pushed me harder, almost knocking me down.

"Sage," he said from a distance, as if performing for a camera. "You're beautiful. So young."

I waited. He was playacting a sexual fantasy in his head. His version of foreplay?

"Sage. I've wanted you since the first moment I saw you. Your beauty outside only matches your beauty inside – you make me dizzy with desire. I dream about holding your body naked against me. Making love . . ."

He sounded like a cheap romance novel and although I knew it was well-rehearsed, I fantasized that it was true. What a scenario. An *older* investigative videographer with obvious sexual prowess, son of The Senator, wanted *me*, a graduate psych student . . .

"Sage, my love," he stepped closer. I didn't move. "So young. So sweet. Say it."

I opened my mouth but no words emerged. He grabbed my shoulders and hissed like a serpent.

"Say it."

My heart raced. I was frightened, aroused, and confused.

"Say it," he shouted.

"Say what?" I whispered.

"You want to fuck me. Now."

"I . . . want to fuck you. Now."

He growled with pleasure and buried his face in my breasts. Then he unbuttoned my shirt and snapped off my bra. He took each breast into his mouth, his tongue sending electric shocks through my body. He toyed with my nipples until they were hard and wildly sensitized. He backed away and led me to the bedroom

The walls were distressed concrete, stained, cracked, and painted a dull grey. A king-sized bed was covered with black satin sheets and a faux zebra skin at the foot. Small mirrors filled the walls and ceilings, in odd, twisted shapes. There was no other furniture. In each corner was a tiny camera – seeing eyes from all angles. He snapped them on from a central switch as we entered the room.

"I don't want to be . . ."

"Sssssssh," he whispered, "it doesn't matter what you want." He peeled off the rest of my clothes and pushed me on to the animal skin. It tickled my back. He stared at my nakedness, not moving. Then he took off his clothes, revealing a huge erection.

I watched him, unable to move.

He spoke without touching me. "I'm going to fuck you kike, like you've never been fucked before."

Before I could respond, he slid on top of me, tracing every part of my body with his fingers, tongue, and penis. I climaxed again and again, reaching dizzying heights that I never experienced. I was putty in his hands; he could do anything. He ran his swollen penis across my face, leaving a sticky trail, and thrust it into my mouth.

He held still – a tremulous moment – and pulled out, hovering over me like a dark shadow.

Suddenly he twisted my arms above my head, grasped my wrists, and plunged into me. Colors burst behind my closed eyelids; my body danced with each thrust. He grunted loudly; the inhuman sounds filled my ears in the same rhythm that he pounded my body.

I screamed. I cried. I was hungry and fevered, lost in his soul.

With a roar that echoed through the room, he finished.

Robert rolled over, leaving me sprawled and dazed.

He took a few minutes to recover. Then he straddled me and smiled, his thighs sticky against my skin. "Not bad for an old man?"

I laughed.

"Thank you. Thank you. Thank you." Robert said smoothly.

He sounded like his father at a fundraiser.

I wanted to protest but his hands and mouth began again, an instant replay that chased all thought from my mind.

Robert could do whatever he wanted.

8

Hours later, I crept from Robert's bed and gathered my clothes. He studied me as I dressed, then smiled and shouted the passwords to the locks on the doors.

I left the man cave without saying a word. Robert turned over and went to sleep.

On the street, I hailed a cab. In the sticky darkness of the back seat, I tried to make sense of our encounter. My mind was screaming – what *happened* and why did I hunger for it? Robert had unearthed a part of me that I never knew existed. I enjoyed sex, but Robert took me to a place I could never imagine.

It was the best sex I ever had. At the same time, it was the strangest sex. I felt both embarrassed and aroused. Wanting more but afraid to pursue my personal *fifty shades of grey.*

I suspected his choreographed fantasy had been played many times before.

I've wanted you since the first moment I saw you. Your beauty outside only matches your beauty inside – you make me dizzy with desire. I dream about holding your body naked against me. Making love . . ."

That didn't disturb me. After all, didn't we all have sexual fantasies that we played out in our minds and bedrooms? Robert was so proficient that I didn't care which movie screened in his head. It was a wild, untamed experience.

I want a rerun.

Yet I couldn't mute the words he spoke right before he mounted me.

I'm going to fuck you kike, like you've never been fucked before.

What was that about? Certainly, it was politically *in*correct – not passionate utterances of The Senator's Son. Or maybe that was precisely The Senator's Son, ridiculing his constituency?

And the cameras?

What was going on in Robert's mind? Was he creating a video montage of his sexual excursions? Would I see myself on You Tube in the morning?

Something told me to run from this man. He was dangerous – unpredictable. I couldn't control him. He was leading me into a slippery and treacherous place.

Black ice.

You can't see it until you slip, careening out of control.

"Be smart," I said out loud, startling the cabbie from his reverie. "Don't go there."

I knew it was only words.

Robert had already snared me.

9

Hanya was pacing the condo when I arrived home.

"Where were you?" She demanded, red-faced.

"At the library."

"With no books? No laptop? No tablet?"

"I . . ."

"I know you're lying, Sage. Can you tell me the truth? Or maybe, you don't want to tell me anything. That's okay. We both know that all of us have our own version of the truth."

I hated when Hanya quoted herself. Did she really believe the hype created by her producers?

"Truth With Dr. H?"

She glared at me.

"I was afraid for you," she said finally. "We don't know what this Mack is capable of – he already shot, maybe killed someone. He sent us messages . . ."

"Why would he care about me?"

"You're one of us."

"Of us?"

"Me. Ayla. Moeda."

"Not really. I'm in the background, remember? The student – intern – who doesn't know very much? The coffee page?"

Hanya was silent. Her face sagged and she looked old and very tired. "I'm scared. For me. For you. For all of us."

I was immediately sorry for being nasty but I hated her self-indulgence, posing as a suffering victim. It didn't match her *Armani*.

There was nothing to say.

"What are you scared of?" Ayla entered the room. How long had she been there?

"Mack." I said quickly.

"Me too. I already know what he's capable of doing."

"We all know that," Hanya said softly. "Let's have some tea and talk."

She led us to the country kitchen table and steeped a pot of mint tea. When it was ready, Hanya placed a steaming mug in front of each of us, along with a small pitcher of cream, a holder with packets of *Splenda* and sugar, and replaced the plate of truffles with an ivory Lenox China bowl filled with buttery *La Maison* toffee.

We drank the tea and savored the candy.

"What next?" Ayla asked.

Hanya and I looked at one another.

"We have to wait," Hanya said, "until the police find Mack."

"What if they don't?"

"Don't think like that. Of course they will."

Ayla shrugged. "He's an old man. No one thinks of an old man as a killer."

"That again," I snapped. "I hate talk like that."

"It's true," Hanya sighed. "Our culture likes to make old people disappear."

"No! Look at you. You're in every paper, on and offline, on all the news. They love you."

"Maybe."

"Of course," Ayla agreed. "But that's not the point. What are *we* going to do *now*?"

The *we* sounded strained as if it didn't quite belong in this conversation. I wondered how Robert would have responded. Or Steen. Suddenly my head filled with a replay of the evening with Robert, and I struggled to attend to the two women drinking tea with me. My body tingled and I wanted him.

"Are you okay?" Hanya asked.

"Of course. Just thinking."

"About what?" Ayla demanded slyly.

"Tomorrow. The next day. How long can we hole up here?"

"Hole up?" Hanya smirked. "You didn't do that earlier."

No, I sure didn't.

"You know what I mean."

Hanya shrugged. "Ayla, why don't we talk about Mack? Who he is – what will he do? Perhaps we can figure out something from what you say and help Steen in his investigation."

"He's horrible," Ayla snarled. "An evil, cruel psychopath. He'll kill and hurt anyone in his way. He made me abandon my baby . . ."

She began to sob.

Big drama. Too big.

Hanya put her hand on the younger woman's shoulder. "It's okay; we don't have to talk about him."

Ayla sobbed louder, her cries echoing in the condo.

"It's okay. It's really okay."

Is it? Or is this outburst a bit too much?

"We're not on TV," I mumbled.

Hanya glared at me.

Ayla pretended not to hear.

10

Four days later Steen called us down to the precinct office to check out his photos. The Detective took a cab through the Manhattan canyons, dwarfed by skyscrapers. I stared at the buildings mirroring each other in the mid-day sun. They looked more like a mirage than steel and glass.

The Detective greeted us, in a rumpled facsimile of the suit he wore when we last met. We wore jeans and simple blouses. Robert followed with Isobel. She was dressed in pink, and studiously taped everything.

I couldn't meet Robert's eyes. Did the others notice? Or did they see him rub up against me in the elevator or squeeze my butt when we were the last two out? Would it show on Isobel's tape?

We were ushered into the captain's office and invited to sit in stiff, regulation chairs – NYPD's idea of luxury – and shown piles of photos, hoping to find a clearer picture of Mack.

Nothing.

Steen thanked us then led the way back to a waiting police van.

"A quick visit to Moeda," he said softly. "Maybe that will shake up some memories."

It was strange climbing into a van marked NYPD, but Steen insisted. He was a formidable force, particularly on his own turf. Hanya studied him, an odd look in her eyes. Before I could analyze what was happening, we were ushered through back doors and elevators to Moeda's floor. The woman, still in ICU, seemed to have shrunk in the last few days. Her body was buried in tubes and sensors; her bed surrounded by monitoring equipment. Ayla gave the requisite screams then buried her head in Moeda's chest.

There was no reaction.

"She remains in a coma," Robert said to the camera. "At this point, her daughter, Dr. H, and Dr. H's great niece, Sage, live in fear of Moeda's alleged attacker. Although there's an NYPD search for Mack, no one has seen him. Hundreds of false reports have come in but nothing offers hard evidence."

Robert magically reframed his face into sad; he half-closed his eyes and spoke in a dramatic whisper.

"How will this story end? Will Moeda win the biggest fight of her life and survive? Will Ayla find her abandoned baby? Will Dr. H return to her show?"

There was a long pause as Isobel panned the room.

"No one knows," Robert said mournfully.

It was contrived to look silly in reality and effective on the screen. What was that about? Robert was very different than the man who called me a kike and ravaged me like a wolf devouring his prey. Steen was evasive, Ayla bored, and Hanya confused.

The day was yet another comedy of errors.

11

We returned to Munsee Court with Robert and Isobel trailing. Steen left us. Tired, but relieved to get the day over, we rode the elevator in silence. I caught Robert's eye. I could see the hunger.

Later.

He mouthed the word and my heart raced.

I followed the women down the hall, trying to rid my mind of the promise in his eyes.

Ayla, Robert, and Isobel entered the living room. I followed. Isobel turned to tape as we collapsed into the couch. She didn't miss a byte.

"Excuse me," Hanya said lightly. She continued down the hall, past Ayla's guest room, my bedroom, and into the master. Hanya could have used the closer bathroom but instead chose her private bath, elegant, veined marble-tiled with tasteful gold fixtures.

I listened to her walk down the hall, stopped at her bedroom, and opened the master bathroom door. Something felt wrong.

As if I knew.

The screams were bloodcurdling.

Dr. H isn't supposed to scream.

I froze, not knowing what to do. The screams were louder, more desperate. I was the first to move, followed by Robert, Ayla and of course, Isobel with her camera.

"Hanya," I screamed. "What's wrong . . . what's happened?"

I found her in the bathroom. Hanya was hysterical.

The marble tiles were streaked with blood. Shiny gold metal pushpins were scattered on the floor. Hanya pointed to the toilet.

Marisol, her Maine Coon, was covered in blood. Pushpins stuck out from all over the cat's body. She was wedged in the toilet bowl, not moving.

"Who did this?" Hanya wailed.

Robert pushed past Hanya. He pulled the limp cat from the bowl. Her fur was matted with blood, her body covered with knife slashes.

"She's dead," Robert said gently.

"Dead," Hanya sobbed. She grabbed the cat from Robert's hands, pressing it against her body. "Dead? Dead? Marisol is dead?"

Another outfit stained with blood.

"Hanya," I said softly. "Let me help you." I touched her arm.

"No," she wrenched herself away from me. "Who would kill Marisol – who would *murder* an innocent cat?"

Hanya crumbled to the floor, sobbing frantically and clinging to the dead animal.

"Who would *want* to kill a cat?" Ayla frowned.

Robert stared at the blood on his hands, a strange smile playing on his face. That's when I noticed it on the mirror, over the sink, and beneath the three gold lamps. The letters were written sloppily in cat's blood. I squinted. At first, I didn't believe what I saw. My heart pounded, my hands balled into fists, my nails dug into my palms.

12

I called Steen. He arrived quickly – perhaps *too* fast, trailed by the crime scene investigation unit. I couldn't quiet Hanya. She sobbed, trembled, and clung to the dead cat like a terrified child.

Steen paused, assessed the scene, and took over. He pried the cat from Hanya's arms, whispering something in her ear. The investigation unit ushered us out of the bathroom. A photographer took shots of the name on the wall. Steen handed off Marisol and draped his arm around Hanya to comfort her. She fell against him sobbing.

"Let's get out of these clothes," I said gently. It felt like déjà vu from when I helped her change out of the bloodied Armani suit at the studio.

Steen pried her off his chest. "Sage will take care of you," he said softly in a tone I thought impossible for a jaded NYPD Detective. "I'll take care of . . . this." There were a few bloodstains on his jacket. I wondered if he would remove them or allow the spatter to become part of the dull, rumpled patina of his suit. Hanya allowed me to lead her into the bedroom and close the door against the mess. We could still hear the voices as I helped her change out of her bloody clothes. Hanya was calmer, her eyes glazed and her lips trembled. Steen knocked at the door.

"Can I talk to all of you? On the couch?"

I looked at Hanya. She bit her lip and nodded.

We headed to the living room, avoiding the chaotic bathroom scene. Tamirah had magically appeared, finding a seat on the couch. How did the woman always *know* when to show up?

Griet and Visch arrived. Robert and Isobel stood, waiting to start taping. Ayla stared absently at her nails.

Hanya and I sat.

Steen asked us each to retell the story. Over and over, in our own words.

Hanya sat quietly, stunned, patting her lap as if expecting Marisol to jump up. She went through an unconscious ritual, searching for her cat. She finally clenched her empty hands. I put my arm around her but she didn't notice.

"This could be a *Lifetime* movie," Griet observed.

When everyone had given their version, Steen related a different story. "The doorman reported that someone called down from the apartment and said it was alright to let the old gentleman in."

"The old gentleman?"

"I assume Mack."

"Who called from the apartment? We were out and . . ."

Steen stared at me coldly. "Someone did it, Sage. Was there a cleaning lady?"

"Yes . . . no . . . maybe. She usually comes today but . . ."

"But what?"

"We were gone before she arrived."

"So who called?"

There was dead silence.

"I believe," Steen said heavily, "that there is more than one person involved in . . . this."

"What?"

Steen repeated himself.

I opened my mouth to argue but no words came. I looked around. Me, Hanya, Ayla, Robert, Griet, Visch, Tamirah . . . could one of *us* be in on this? Who had a motive and at the same time, who *didn't* have a motive?

Everyone looked uncomfortable and guilty.

Except for Robert.

"How could it be one of us?" Ayla whined. "Would I shoot my mother? Would I kill a cat?"

Hanya shuddered.

Ayla's words were followed by a chorus of denials.

"Shut up!" Steen shouted. "It doesn't help."

There was an uneasy hush. I stared at my blue-painted fingernails. It had to be one of us here. The thought was terrifying. If the assailant or the assailant's assistant was among us, then he or she fooled everyone.

Including me.

I thought of Robert.

Kike.

Did he hate Jews? Hanya and I weren't religious but we were still Jewish, with a Sephardic genealogy we could trace back to the 15th century. Was this another scenario created by Robert?

My thoughts were broken by images of his love-making. If he hated me why did he perform like that?

"Don't start making judgments," Steen said firmly, as if reading my thoughts. "Leave that to me."

Ayla?

She certainly had cause. Get rid of Moeda, collect her inheritance, and ride off with Mack like she had so many years ago.

Hanya?

I didn't think my aunt was capable of organizing such evil. Yet she *was* a media psychologist, constantly in search of a good story. Hanya would never murder her cat. That required the flair of a psychopath.

Griet?

The ratings would skyrocket. She had insisted on taping everything, using The Senator's Son as her famous investigative videographer . . .

Visch?

The attorney collaborating with Griet?

Steen tapped me on the shoulder. I looked up, not realizing that everyone was staring at me.

"You're all suspects," he stared into my eyes, speaking slowly as if on a TV crime drama. "Until one-by-one you're ruled out."

"Me?" It never occurred to me that I could be a suspect.

Hanya unconsciously leaned away from me. My arm fell from her shoulders.

"Me?" I said again.

Steen studied my face.

"It would be convenient," Ayla began. "And Mack would like your type – young and pretty."

I stared, dumbfounded, at her piercing blue eyes. Weren't they always flat and somewhat glazed?

"How can you . . ."

Steen stopped me. "Let's not jump to any conclusions. We don't know anything yet."

"She could have let him into the apartment – after all, she let in the envelope" Ayla continued defiantly. "Sage could have planted Mack in the audience, sent the texts . . ."

"Me?" I repeated stupidly. "How would I know the envelope was filled with talcum powder?"

Robert tried to stop Ayla's tirade. "Don't be ridiculous, Ayla. Why would Sage do that to her aunt? She loves Hanya like a mother."

"So it seems," Ayla said acidly. "Good ratings . . . drama. Sage would be helping her aunt and herself."

"For all we know," Robert continued, "it was *you*."

"Me? Shoot my mother? After all these years I found her and . . ."

Robert shook his head, cutting her off. "We all know that you're no innocent."

"Maybe it was *you*, Robert." Hanya said in a trembling voice.

He grinned at the idea of being a suspect. "That's ridiculous."

"Is it? All of this makes your great investigative videography into an award winning documentary." Her voice grew stronger. "Maybe a feature film after that."

"Hanya," I said firmly. "It wasn't Robert."

"How do you know?"

Because he's the greatest lover I ever had?

"I just know."

Robert thanked me by slowly running the tip of his tongue between his lips.

"Enough," Steen said tiredly. "Leave it to forensics – we'll figure it out. Right now it's been more than enough for one day. The crime scene people will be gone soon."

Hanya nodded. "I need to lie down," she said softly. "Sage, will you come with me?"

"Of course." I stood up. As she turned her back, Robert held up his phone and mouthed, "I'll text you."

Only Isobel saw.

I nodded.

Ayla headed for her bedroom.

Griet and Visch consulted by the window.

As I led Hanya away, I turned around. Steen saw Robert hold up his phone. He glanced at Hanya, an unreadable expression on his face. He and I both followed Tamirah's surreptitious exit from the scene, clutching her briefcase and saying nothing.

I caught Steen looking at me. He was trying to say something.

Hanya grabbed my hand. "Sage, *now.*"

I turned away as Steen mouthed two words that made me shiver. *Watch out.*

13

Robert texted to meet in front of the dive bar.

Hanya took a sleeping pill and remained in her bedroom until the next morning. Sleep was her drug of choice. Ayla stared at the flat screen TV in her bedroom. Griet and Visch finally left together for an expensive meal at *Le Bernadin* on West 51st, and then back to the studio offices.

Everyone was quiet and settled for the moment. Steen's warning haunted me.

Watch out.

Watch out for what? For whom? I couldn't sleep, study or even concentrate on mindless TV. Even the *Property Brothers* and *Modern Family* eluded me. I texted Robert.

I'm leaving.

No one noticed when I took the elevator and had Remez hail a cab. I was on my own, which was exactly what I wanted. Press, bloggers, judgmental viewers, and tell-it-all "friends" never noticed my escape. I was a minor supporting actor in the drama. The cab arrived and it felt other-worldly, as if my life had shifted into a new dimension.

Robert was waiting for me on the street. I paid the cabbie and walked over to Robert, as if in a dream. He didn't speak. Suddenly he grabbed me, covering my mouth. I tried to scream but he pushed me into a narrow alley, pinning me against the wall. I squirmed but he was too strong – I was helpless against him.

"I'm going to fuck you," he whispered in my ear.

I was filled with a mix of fear and arousal, enveloped by my own movie.

"Play the game," Robert hissed. "You know how."

"What game?"

He bit my neck. "*This* game."

"I'm not in the mood," I struggled against his grip. "Too much has happened."

"That's exactly why you're in the mood."

He pressed his body against me.

"Fight me Sage and I'll kill you."

I struggled to free myself but his legs held me firm against the wall. He twisted my arms behind my back. Then he slapped me lightly across my face.

"Whore," he whispered gleefully.

I was stunned.

He grabbed my throat. "Fight me and I'll kill you." He tightened his grip. "I'll let you go when you calm down. I'm going to fuck you either way."

Suddenly I was afraid. A few college guys glanced down the alley.

"You okay?" one asked.

"She's okay," Robert laughed. "Just practicing lines for an audition." He released my arms and stepped back.

"I'm asking *her*," the beefiest kid took a step into the alley.

"I'm fine," I rubbed my wrists. "Just rehearsing.

The guys got it. They were probably NYU students. "If you need us, give a yell," the beefy guy said.

"We can play the cops," another called.

They laughed and walked away.

Robert grinned. "Now wasn't that fun?"

I stared at him, still flat against the wall.

"Wasn't that fun?" He repeated.

I couldn't move. Who was this man?

"Oh baby, I know you *liked* that."

It was bizarre. I struggled to make sense of him, what had just happened, *and* me. Was I afraid? Did I like it? As if to answer my question, Robert leaned over and kissed me lightly on the lips. He moved to my neck and to my ear. "Role playing," he explained. "That's my next lesson."

I tried to speak but there were no words. "Come on, Sage, lighten up. Let's have a drink and then we can go back to my place . . ."

He took my hand and led me out of the alley to the sidewalk. "Let's have some microbrew," he grinned.

I numbly followed him into the bar.

14

"I know you liked it," Robert said later, lying naked next to me on his bed.

"I didn't."

He laughed. We had just finished an hour of outrageous sex. He had been aroused by the gameplay on the street and the noise in the bar, showing it by twisting me into an array of Kama sutra positions like the statues on the shelf.

I was crazed, I was frightened, and I was confused. He awakened something in me that lied in wait – a memory of violence and treachery that followed me like wolves and humans in early history. What was it about me – my family – that was compelled to attract predators? Was there a past; a flawed genealogy fraught with unconscious memories and terrors?

Some called it genetic memory – a memory at birth that had been incorporated into the genetic code; unconscious behavior that compelled one to respond in a certain manner. Carl Jung spoke about *collective unconscious* – feelings and ideas inherited from our ancestors. Even some parapsychologists suggested that experiences can be encoded in genes.

It always sounded speculative – ideas that are fun to consider but unsupported by science, logic, and experience.

What if I was wrong? What if they weren't conjectures but truths about our reality?

I looked at Robert. Perhaps I was drawn to him because of deeply embedded genetic memories? Or maybe it was a simpler answer. Joshua. I was psychologically seduced by my evil cousin, early-on, when everyone else around me was afraid of him. Even Grandma Espie had warned me. Her words haunted my memory.

"Joshua ran away, Grandma," I wailed. *"He ran away from* me.*"*
"I'm sorry, so very sorry."
"I don't understand."
"None of us understands."

Was that why she gave me the hamsa? Was Robert another Joshua . . . another Mack?

Truth With Dr. H! did a slow rerun in my head.

"Is Mack a psychopath?" Hanya asked.

Ayla looked at her blankly. "What's a psychopath?"

"In the early 19th century, the word psychopath described a person who was normal on the outside and morally depraved on the inside. Today, many people think of a psychopath as someone who murders without feeling and a sociopath for those who have no feeling. Essentially, both are callous, uncaring with a total lack of empathy. They have little or no emotions, blaming others for things that are their fault – often using language that cons people into believing their lies. Like the psychopath who murders a stranger on the street. 'They made me do it,' would be the explanation."

Hanya continued. "They're often overconfident – grandiose – impulsive, self-centered, and generally unable to plan for the future. They lie, manipulate, and wreak havoc on those around them. They don't care about you. Many are violent – abusive – and have no tolerance for frustration. Many are charming, glib – able to fake love for blood. They can hurt, maim, and kill without a care in the world."

"Mack?" Ayla whispered.

"Robert?" I said out loud to the man next to me in bed.

Robert laughed louder. "What?"

"Stop . . . everything."

"There's no stopping now, love. You'll see. Once in motion, life grinds on until it's satisfied."

"I don't understand," I begged for empathy. "There's so much going on – the shooting, the fake ricin, the threats, Marisol – what next?"

"Me," Robert said quickly and mounted me. "Thank you. Thank you. Thank you."

The psychopaths and wolves muted beneath my arousal. Robert caressed them away with the finesse of a Casanova – the infamous 18th century Italian known for his elaborate affairs. Casanova, who wrote in his memoirs, without remorse:

I have delighted in going astray . . . cultivating whatever gave pleasure to my senses was always the chief business of my life

Who was Robert – Casanova, psychopath, or both? Were all the men in my life – in my genealogy – the same? Briefly, my head was filled with names I didn't recognize – Dutch, Spanish, and Portuguese danced in my mind. Who were they? Where did they come from? Why now?

I forced myself back into Robert's bizarre love-making. The names didn't disappear. I knew that they had surfaced, determined to remain. Why? The hamsa told me.

It was time.

15

It took four days. Something in my head demanded action. Where did it come from? The hamsa? My subconscious? I don't exactly why, but twelve days after Moeda was shot, I knew it was *time*.

I had to figure out what was happening to us. I couldn't get past Marisol's murder. It reminded me of a stray dog from my childhood. Joshua called him *Dog* and he lived in the park near my house. One day someone trapped and burned Dog to death. I was horrified – and now, someone did that to a creature in my home. I had done nothing as a child but cry and rail against evil people.

I was no longer a child.

Sublimate – a voice inside me instructed. Transform sexual energy into something productive and concrete. Perhaps if I could solve today's mystery, I would be able to go back and understand Joshua and the other men who peopled my history.

I decided to open my own investigation without telling anyone. My plan was to gather facts and share them with Steen.

I went through the sliding glass doors in the living room and on to the terrace. It was a huge space, running a full 50 feet along the side of the condo. The floor was tiled in outdoor terra cotta; the railing was clear with decorative iron posts. Carriage lights hung along the wall and Hanya had filled the space with several wrought iron tables and chairs, plants, and a small standing sculpture of Peter Stuyvesant.

"Why would you want Stuyvesant on your terrace?" I once asked Hanya.

"It's a copy of the bronze statue in Stuyvesant Square," she explained. "Stuyvesant stands there with his peg-leg, haughty and uncompromising. Perhaps the way he looked when our ancestors came from Recife, Brazil. I keep him here to remind me that Jews had to *fight* to live on this very street."

At the time, I wondered why it was so important for Hanya to connect with the past. Who cared about Peter Stuyvesant and New Amsterdam? Until the shooting, the present occupied all of my time. The strange names I had heard when I lay with Robert danced in my head. They were no longer the past.

"It's who we are," Hanya explained.

"Who we are? Does anyone know? "

"We can't let go," Hanya insisted. "They live inside us."

There was no logic. I was a scientist not a novelist. Life was about *today*. Yesterday was finished. Peg-leg Stuyvesant was a legend in the past.

"Yesterday is never over," Hanya told me softly.

I shrugged, staring at the skyscrapers that enveloped our terrace. Suddenly my hamsa burned. Grandma Espie's words whispered in my mind, as if she were there, on the terrace, talking to me.

"I have something for you."

She opened the chain that held the hamsa on her neck.

"It's protected me all my life. My mother told me the story. The hamsa is ancient – some say it represents the hand of Miriam. Others say it's the sister of Moses. They all know it's the protective hand of God. It draws positive energy – life and happiness – and repels the evil eye and the angel of death. The hamsa served me well. Mother gave it to me – and her mother gave it before that. Hundreds of years reaching back to Esperanza, our ancestor who was expelled from Spain."

She put the hamsa on my neck.

"Esperanza – the one with red hair and hazel eyes. The same as our red hair and hazel eyes. Esperanza's spirit is in this . . . Mother's spirit . . . and mine. We'll protect you from wherever we are. When it's your time, give it to someone you love very much. Someone who needs its protection."

The hamsa had been in New Amsterdam with Peter Stuyvesant and the others. Now it was going to help me find the people who threatened us today.

It was silly, magical thinking but the hamsa seemed to know what I was thinking and confirmed my decision.

I stared at the moonrise. It had been the same, hundreds of years ago, hiding old secrets I couldn't fathom. The moon stared back at me, waiting for the truth.

Not Dr. Hanya's truth.

16

I began with the cleaning lady, Mallah. She had stringy brown hair, a short thick body, and almost-black eyes. She worked hard and spoke little, cleaning twice a week without anyone noticing her.

"Where were you when Marisol was killed?" I asked lightly.

Mallah raised her eyes from the dishes in the sink and stared at me. "I do nothing wrong," she said defiantly.

"I'm not saying that you did. I just want to know."

She shrugged her shoulders and returned to the dishes. "Whoever killed that cat is evil. Very evil. Evil *in* this house."

She crossed herself, detergent bubbles falling across her smock. "Evil."

I backed away.

She was right. *Evil*. I thought of Dr. Robert Hare, the psychologist who was the first to accurately define psychopath, suggesting there are millions of them living among us – not always murderers. He pointed out that psychopaths showed such traits as:

lack of remorse or empathy
shallow emotions
manipulativeness
lying
egocentricity
glibness
low frustration tolerance
episodic relationships
parasitic lifestyle
persistent violation of social norms

A grinning skull filled my mind's eye.

Didn't everyone know a psychopath? They were all around us – maybe it was a relative, friend, or neighbor? Maybe it was a therapist who loved stories about serial killers, or a reader who prowled dark minds in his ebook?

I smiled sourly. Most people didn't get it – they preferred to use media definitions. The concept was simple – all killers aren't psychopaths and all psychopaths aren't killers. A psychopath might live next door or be a CEO. He or she might be a successful doctor or filmmaker, politician or wealthy businessman like Robert Moses or Bernie Madoff. Their crimes were cold-blooded; they felt excitement rather than guilt. They exposed themselves through control and manipulation – predators who live among us.

Mallah said it right – evil. Too often, their charm, which is essentially play-acting, convinces us of a very different intent until something happens.

Mallah started mumbling something in Spanish. It sounded like a prayer to protect herself against evil. The same job as my hamsa. Shaking my head, I headed for the elevator. My next target was Remez, the doorman

17

Remez looked like a horror flick version of a charismatic psychopath.

Dressed spotlessly in a doorman's uniform, he smiled, said the right words, spoke evenly and obsequiously. None of it touched his flat eyes. His smile appeared painted; a convenient design for his face.

"I don't know anything, ma'am," he said evenly, hailing a cab.

"I do my job," he added woodenly as he helped a woman carry packages to the elevator.

"Then how did someone get *in*?" I persisted.

"I do my job."

"Who called from the apartment? To let the elderly gentleman in?"

He shrugged. "I get a call, I open the door. Simple. No questions. I'm paid not to ask any questions."

His dark eyes were blank.

"Did you know . . .?"

"I know nothing, ma'am. That's my job. To know nothing. And let . . . bitches . . . excuse me . . . people like you tell me what to do."

"What did you call me?"

"I didn't call you anything."

He grinned.

"I'm going to tell my aunt . . ."

"Tell her what? That I called her spoiled brat a bitch? I never called you that . . . it was a general term, understand? Of course you understand, ma'm. I was referring to the little white Bichon Frise that lives in 3a. She *is* a bitch, you know. All female dogs are bitches . . ."

I grimaced.

"Can I help you with anything else?" He asked sweetly.

I made a mental note. Take Mallah off my list of suspects and add Remez.

I headed uptown, transferring at Grand Central Station to the #6.

18

My next interview took place in the hospital.

Moeda was still in a coma. I wasn't sure what I expected to find, but I had to try. She was in an intensive care cubicle surrounded by monitors, tubes, and sensors protruding from all over her body. A white sheet and thin blanket covered her; arms were placed next to her body, sporting an assortment of connections.

The ICU was incredibly noisy. As I made my way to her room, I listened to the ongoing emergencies in the unit – cardiac arrests, pulmonary failure, and deaths of people with DNRs – Do Not Resuscitate orders. Part of me wanted to peek into every room and learn the stories of the people in the beds – the ones hovering close to death, and those watching.

What did it feel like? What were they thinking? I recalled stories of near-death experiences where people saw a light and loved ones who had passed before them. The loved ones invariably turned them away.

It's not your time.

Later they learned that they "died" on a surgery table or in a car accident and were resuscitated. I wondered if I experienced near-death, would I find the psychopaths in my history waving me back or forward?

That made me smile.

I was equally fascinated by the visitors, pale-faced and hunched, waiting for something to change. Who were they and why did they care so much? Were there psychopaths hidden behind frowns? Ted Bundy, who confessed to 30 murders right before his 1989 execution, described himself as *"the most cold-hearted son of a bitch you'll ever meet,"* was expert at faking any normal human emotion, deceiving everyone around him.

Was I being deceived?

Doctors, nurses, and other medical staff were a blur of activity, chasing visitors out during "procedures," sharing information, comforting loved ones. It was the dramatic heart of our times, steeped in antiseptics and efficiency, technology roaring like a critter suddenly released from its cage with nowhere and everywhere to go.

I nodded as Moeda's nurse left the room.

No one questioned who I was.

I leaned against Moeda's bedrail and stared at the unconscious woman.

"What happened?" I asked softly. "Why?"

There was no response.

GSW – that's what Steen called it – gunshot wound. The bullet had entered through her forehead and exited through the side of her head, splattering blood over Hanya's *Armani* suit. It wasn't a deep wound but her coma indicated potential brain damage. What would be left if and when she came out of the coma? Would Moeda suffer cognitive impairment and physical disabilities? Would the shooting erase all memory of what happened seconds before? Would she survive at all?

"I wish you could answer my questions, Moeda," I said gently to the woman.

Did her eyelids flutter or was it my imagination?

"Was it *him*?" I persisted. Perhaps she would give me another sign. "Was there someone involved who you knew? Who Ayla knew?"

Moeda remained still.

Suddenly, unfamiliar words emerged. I don't know where they came from. My hamsa felt warm against my skin.

Eil na rafa na la
Please, God, Please heal her

I knew what they meant as soon as I spoke them. It was Moses' simple prayer for his very sick sister, Miriam. I thought of Moses and his protégé, Joshua. Always Joshua – seeping into my consciousness. Would I ever erase that image?

It was strange – almost magical. I wasn't a practicing Jew – the only religious person in my family was Grandma Espie. So why *now*? Was it still part of me, buried inside the 90 percent of the brain we don't use, waiting to surface like a magical clue to the past? A companion to the others, shrouded in mystery?

I shivered. There was so much I didn't know. So much that no one knew.

And so much that people like Mack and Moeda *knew* but wouldn't tell.

19

My last stop was Steen.

John Steen was a man who could be trusted. I sat on a hard, wood chair next to his desk. The desk was piled with papers and folders; the surrounding room noisy with other detectives, telephones, computers, and too many people.

I told him about my investigation.

"That's not smart," Steen chewed on a pencil thoughtfully. "You should leave it to us."

I shrugged.

"Mack is a predator," Steen leaned closer. "A dangerous man."

"A psychopath," I corrected, flaunting my knowledge like a first grader reading big words.

Steen smiled. "That's true, Sage. "But you need to understand . . . perhaps a less clinical and more forensic fact."

"What's that?"

"God gave us this . . ." He touched his heart. "And this," he touched his head. "Within all of us he left sparks of evil."

"I don't understand."

"Potential for evil." Steen scowled. "You have it. I have it. We all own it, deep inside."

I smirked. Was The Detective trying to teach me about Freud's id? "What makes us different?"

"We control it. We stop it. We layer it between morality and ethics. We pretend it's not there, it doesn't exist. But it's *always* there. That's why we love to watch it on TV or in the movies, and read about it in books and newspapers. We tamed our impulses and live vicariously through the murderers and serial killers in our media lives."

"And the predator?"

"He has none of that. He only pretends to care – see wrong – pretends to be *human*. He professes compassion but is true evil. He feels nothing – he's an actor covering up the evil that permeates his soul."

"Do I detect a bit of . . . religion?"

"No," Steen shook his head sadly. "You detect a lot of experience."

He had me there.

"He'll strike again and again until he's stopped. He's been doing it his entire life."

"Mack? That explains Ayla, the biker gang, and perhaps bodies he left behind during his lifetime."

"Yes, Sage. It explains them and many others in my world."

Suddenly there was a shift in time. Steen's face changed but didn't – the same man in a different context – wearing wool breeches and a thick leather belt with a deerskin pouch and hunting knife. Thick dark hair covered his body, along with a bushy beard and mustache that made him look fierce.

I tried to shake the image from my mind.

"Are you okay?"

"Yes." My words were awkward, confused. "If I see . . . get close . . . to Mack, I'll contact you immediately."

Who was the man in wool breeches?

"It's not just Mack I'm worried about."

Deerskin pouch and hunting knife? In New York City?

"Are you with me Sage?"

"Yes, of course. You wanted to know?"

Steen took a deep breath, studying my face. "It's not just Mack I'm worried about," he repeated.

The image faded, replaced by the skull.

My heart raced and my hands trembled. I tried not to let Steen see. "Who are you worried about?" I asked, my voice defiant.

"His accomplice," Steen responded quickly. "Maybe he or she is also a psychopath . . . and maybe not. We don't know. The only thing we know is there's someone else who thinks that they're helping Mack by hurting us."

I nodded. "This can be very dangerous."

"It's a big unknown, Sage. We don't even have any real clues. Just implications about someone else helping Mack."

I took a deep breath. "I'll be careful."

"I don't want you putting yourself in danger. That's not the point of all this. We need to apprehend Mack, find his accomplice, and hopefully, get Moeda well."

"Hopefully."

Steen sighed. "It looks bad. No one knows . . . a bullet in the brain . . . there are miracles every day. There are also famous impaired people like Gabrielle Giffords who, has said among other things, that her injury took away her "gift of speech.""

I filled in the rest. "And those who never recover – who remain in a coma for their entire lives, which are usually not that long."

We were silent.

"No one knows the future," Steen said sadly. "Only God."

Or the past?

"Who is God, Detective? Christian, Jewish, Muslim, Hindu . . . which God wins?"

Steen smiled. "You remind me of my daughter."

"Is that good?"

"Very good."

"Then I'll take the compliment."

"With it comes the worry. Please, Sage, be careful. You don't know what kind of swamp you're entering."

"I promise," I said lightly.

I left the precinct. I was halfway down the block before I began to tremble. How did this happen? Why *us*? Where was it all going? Where was it coming from?

I needed to talk. I pulled out my cell and he picked up on the third ring.

"Robert," I said breathlessly, "can I see you?"

20

We sat in a noisy *Starbucks* filled with people and the enticing scent of fresh coffee. I drank a mocha cookie crumble. Robert sipped a large black coffee, no milk or sugar.

Robert didn't like chocolate.

We looked at each other silently. He waited for me to speak.

"I'm scared," I began.

Robert sandwiched my hand between his. Our eyes met.

"Tell me," he said in a soap opera voice.

I told him. I described the cleaning lady, doorman, Moeda, and Steen. I talked about what Steen had said and speculated on the nature of a psychopath. I didn't mention the image of the man in wool breeches or the skull.

He listened silently. When I was finished, he took a deep breath.

"What you need, Sage, is a diversion from all this."

"A diversion?"

"Something to get your mind off this seedy stuff."

"I don't understand."

He licked his lips. "Come with me," he stood and took my hand. "We're going to have some fun."

I wondered if he heard me – understood my fears?

Did it matter?

Robert led me down the street, dodging people, dogs, and messengers. We were heading for his apartment.

"Sex," Robert said softly. "It always makes you feel better."

21

This was the strangest role playing yet. I tried to figure out Robert's intent – analyze his fantasy, but in the end, I came up blank. Was it the effect of growing up as the son of a political celebrity? Did The Senator have similar, bizarre tastes? Or did this belong solely to Robert? I had no answers, only questions, so I followed his lead.

Robert placed us in the middle of his darkened man cave. We faced each other, fully clothed.

Robert circled me like a cat cornering his prey.

"Hit me," he ordered.

"No."

"Hit me," he growled, waving his hands in my face.

"I can't . . .

"Fucking whore," he grabbed my wrists. "If you don't hit me, I'll hit you."

The calm in his eyes didn't match the fire in his voice. "I can't do . . ."

Suddenly Robert pushed me hard, making me stumble. He thrust his face into mine, daring me. "Slap me, hit me, hurt me. Do it. *Do it.*"

I raised my hand, suffocated by his ferocity.

"*Do it!*"

A game, I thought. This is all a game to take my mind off of Mack and his accomplice. Isn't that what Robert said?

"This will take your mind off the seedy stuff."

I slapped him softly.

"Harder, kike. It has to hurt."

I always hated the word kike. It made me think of white supremacists living in Montana woods, carrying AK-47s, wearing army boots and camouflage clothes.

"Don't call me a kike," I shouted.

"Then fucking hit me like you mean it."

I hit his chest so hard that both of us were stunned. We stared at one another. Moving like a serpent cornering its prey, Robert caught my arms and twisted. Then he kicked my legs until I collapsed to the floor. He bent down and pinned me with one knee.

"I don't like this."

"Then punch me."

"I want to stop."

"Show me."

He released one arm. I hit him with my fist. He laughed. I hit him harder and he grabbed both arms and pinned them beneath my body. He leaned over and quietly whispered in my ear.

"This is just a game, Sage. Go with it."

Go with what?

I didn't like the game but it was too late. I couldn't move. Robert ripped off my clothes. I screamed. The louder I got, the more he enjoyed it.

"I'm going to fuck you," he snarled. "Fight me whore and I'll kill you."

I struggled wildly.

He slapped me across my breasts. "Whore," he cried gleefully. He kissed me, plunging his tongue into my mouth. I groaned. Everything and everyone left my mind.

Robert grabbed my throat. "Fight me and I'll kill you. I'm going to fuck you dead or alive."

And he said those all too familiar words.

"I'm going to fuck you like you've never been fucked before. And when I finish, you know what you're going to say my Jewish whore? Thank you. Thank you. Thank you." Robert laughed maniacally. He forced my legs apart. His breath was so loud it sounded like a raging wind.

"No," I cried weakly.

I loved the game and hated it. I heard Steen in my head.

Within all of us, God left sparks of evil.

Was this my evil?

Robert bit my neck and plunged into me, grunting like an animal. I climaxed over and over. Robert finished with a howl like a wolf.

22

We lay quietly, naked, on the floor.

"What was *that*?" I asked, my voice hoarse from screaming.

"Rape fantasy," Robert smiled. "Isn't it great?"

"I'm not sure."

"You had no objections while we were doing it."

"I know but . . ."

"Maybe next time you'll rape me. That might be fun."

"I couldn't . . ."

"Of course you can, Sage. You can do anything you want. Just let your id go viral."

I thought of Steen again.

Potential for evil. You have it. I have it. We all own it, deep within.

Was this what Steen was talking about?

I looked into Robert's eyes. He was unmoved by the scene we just enacted. Was it violence? Was it sex? Was it history?

We control our evil. We stop it. We layer it between morality and ethics. We pretend it's not there, it doesn't exist. But it's always there. That's why we love to watch it on TV, the movies, read about it in books. We have tamed our impulses and live vicariously through the murderers and serial killers in our media lives.

And Robert?

The psychopath feels nothing – he's an actor covering up the evil that permeates his soul.

Was Robert a psychopath? I peered into his eyes for proof. The blue was blank, almost icy. No response but a hard stare.

"Robert?" I asked shakily.

"What my love," he said smoothly. "Are you beginning to see the light?"

"I'm not sure . . ."

He laughed and patted my breasts. "You're learning very quickly. If you don't see it today, I'm sure you'll get it tomorrow. It's in your head. Your body has already shown you what it likes – what turns you on."

"I . . ."

"Ssssh," he said and kissed me gently on the lips. "You think too much."

He lay back, his eyes closed. I watched Robert drift off to sleep, his chest moving rhythmically. Who was this man? How many faces did he have? What did he bring out in me?

The third question was the most sobering.

Was Robert the accomplice?

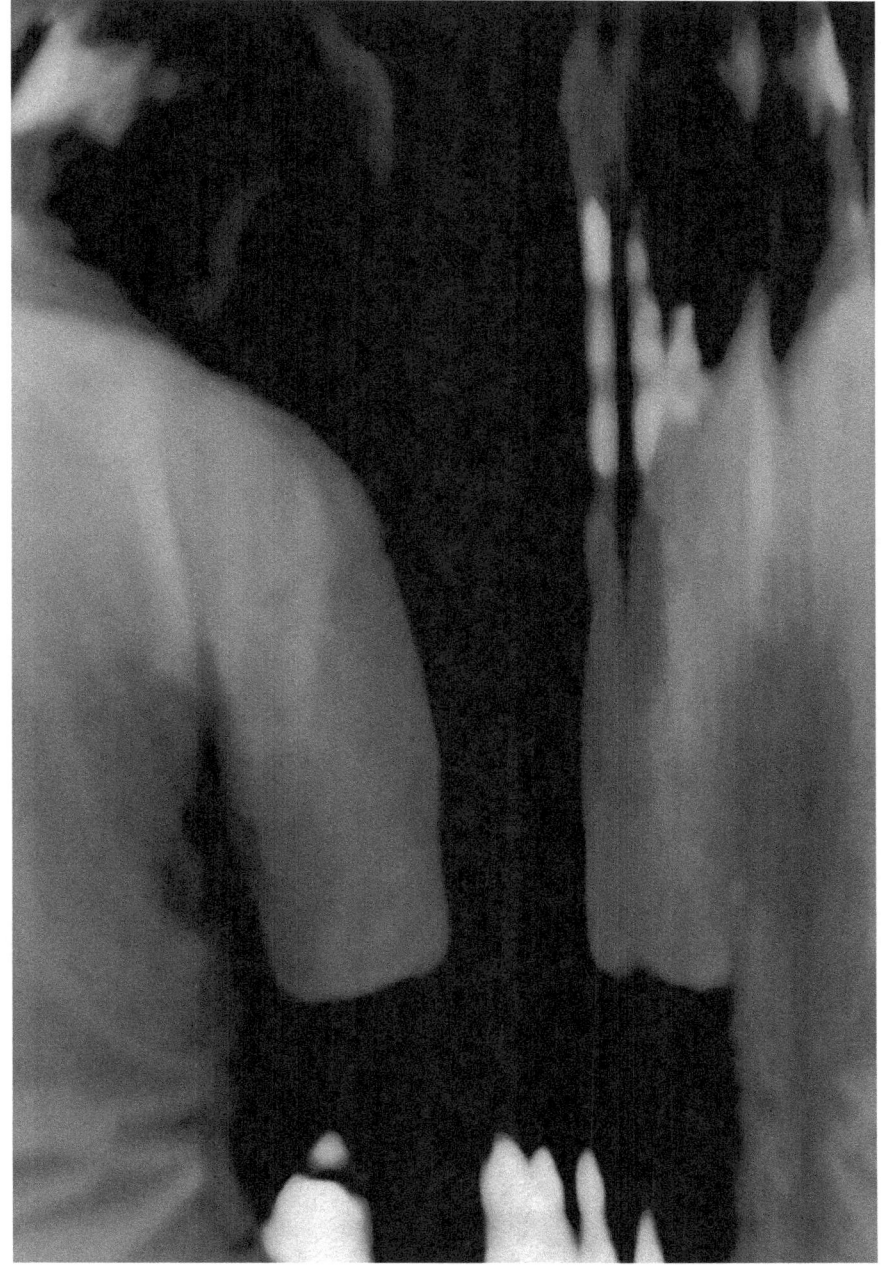

Hanya

1

Sage thought she was fooling me.

There wasn't much she could hide, including Robert. I didn't understand what my intelligent, beautiful grandniece saw in the narcissistic man 23 years her senior. He was flat, with plastic charm promoted by his father for political gain. I'm sure Robert never went knocking on doors to secure contracts and assignments. All he had to do was use his father's name – everyone in New York *loved* The Senator – and no one would turn him away. Robert, with his damn camera, awful questions, and wimpy pink assistant, Isobel, followed us like stray dogs hungry for footage.

The story was big. It had been two weeks since the shooting and the story was still hot. Each byte found its way into the media. If I wanted to know what was happening with *Truth With Dr. H!* all I had to do was turn on a talk show or log onto the Internet. Murder, sex, sordid stories, questionable people, and psychopathic old men were great for business.

The problem was that nothing *else* was happening in my life. I was scared, bored, and tired of entertaining Ayla. Moeda was still in a coma. I needed to go back to work but Griet was adamant. We were on hiatus. I began to think about other things happening in my life like Sage coming home with her face flushed, smelling of sex. I went through her list of potential lovers. There were a lot of names but most she found boring. Sage liked being on the edge – perhaps the result of her childhood friendship with Joshua? That was when I realized it was Robert. Sage didn't just sleep with anyone. She loved notoriety. *Behind the camera* notoriety. I could see her strolling through the Upper East Side, secretly smiling when someone saw she was with the son of The Great Senator.

Unfortunately, Sage routinely chose the wrong man.

Joshua was her first love *and* disaster. I never liked the kid. I told Espie, but my sister refused to listen. I knew it from the first time I met him as a toddler. Joshua was bad.

That was years ago – years that Sage and I chose to forget. We never talked about it. When Sage finally left for college, she began to sleep around. It was predictable. All the guy had to do was offer her chocolate – *good* chocolate – and Sage jumped into bed.

It wasn't that Sage was a sex addict – she hungered for intimacy like she hungered for chocolate. Ironically, she never found it except with me, her spinster aunt who loved her more than anything and anyone in the world. I replaced my sister.

I knew Sage was charmed when Robert arrived with a box of *La Maison Du Chocolat*. If he had brought *Whitman's Sampler* or *Russell Stover* it would have been different. Instead, he arrived with the best chocolate on the planet. Sage knew *that* all too well. Robert could have just flung her on my living room floor and taken her with all of us watching.

Sage had a serious history with chocolate.

It started with her beloved Grandma Espie, my sister. When Mother got sick, Espie brought her chocolate. Cheap stuff but Mother loved it. After Mother died, when Sage was old enough, Espie played the same chocolate game with her. They both loved it.

I *hated* chocolate.

Sage, in turn, gave Joshua chocolate, but he hated it too. In fact, Sage had different kinds of chocolate picked out for everyone in the family.

Except for me.

"I don't bring you chocolate, Hanya," Sage admitted sadly. "Because I know you don't like it."

She was a young teenager and I saw the question in her eyes.

How can you hate chocolate and be human?

It was like hating life.

She brought me mocha-flavored tea instead. I hated that too but never told her.

Sometimes I caught Sage and Espie "trading chocolates" and discussing the qualities of each. I never got the game. Maybe it was because Sage and Espie shared the "family treasure" – red hair, hazel eyes, and the hamsa?

I shrugged. The damn hamsa. As a clinical psychologist, I knew that these things were important in the genealogical life of a family. I often traced behaviors and physical features back hundreds of years to help my patients, discovering family traits and experiences.

I refused to do that with my own family.

Perhaps if I had been less stubborn, things would have turned out differently.

2

I stood in Griet's office, arguing.

"How long are you going to keep me off the air?"

It had been two weeks since Moeda was shot. I knew it would take at least that time to start up.

Griet shrugged. "Sit down, Hanya. We're talking about danger."

"We're talking about *my* show."

"It's my show too."

I sat in the hard chair that Griet kept in her office. The space was decorated to look like it was plucked from a sci-fi movie. They called it post-modern. Nothing was soft or pretty, only hard angles, stone, thick glass, and stainless steel. White was the dominant color, splattered with occasional red. I hated it.

Griet stood up and went to the glass wall. She could see everything that was going on in the studio but no one could see her through the one-way glass. Although a professed post-modernist, Griet never quite trusted the glass. She lowered the white shade as Robert signaled to turn on the camera.

"He's a pain in the ass," I commented.

"If FRS wants him, FRS gets him."

I nodded.

And Sage.

Griet moved from the wall to her desk, a thick slab of clear glass perched atop two sharply angled pyramids of veined white marble. Her only concession to tradition was her plush-cushioned red leather desk chair.

She sat.

I perched on one of the two matching red chairs on the other side of the desk and waited for Griet to get settled.

"Can we speak openly? Between professionals?" Griet narrowed her eyes as if squinting into the future.

"Of course."

"We're scripting everything."

"Scripting?"

"Yes. When this is over . . . and it's just beginning . . . *Truth With Dr. H!* will be bigger than *Ellen* and *The View* combined."

"I don't understand."

Griet tilted her head to the now obscured Robert. "We'll have a *Lifetime* movie. A book. No, a few books, telling their stories. A documentary. Shows focusing on maligned women. Don't you see – it's a blockbuster?"

I knew she was right but I still argued. "I'm not so sure. People forget quickly . . ."

Griet's eyes sparkled. "We won't *let* them forget."

"What are you planning?"

She shrugged.

"You can't leave me out of the loop."

"If I let you in, it wouldn't be reality."

"Reality?"

"Reality TV, Hanya. Don't you see the power of a respected media psychologist going through this? There's no woman who wouldn't drool to learn more."

"You're using me for ratings?"

"*Our* ratings and earnings. Dollars, Hanya. Money."

"Why is it so important?"

There was a tense pause.

"Our ratings are dropping. Remember our plan, Hanya? Bringing Mack to the studio was supposed to help turn the tide and now we have the opportunity . . ."

I took a deep breath. "How can I forget? Does it mean that I have to suffer publicly?"

"You react naturally," Griet smiled. "That's all we ask."

"Who is *we*?"

"That doesn't matter."

"One question. Is that why you brought Mack in for the show?"

Anger flashed in Griet's eyes.

"You're dealing with peoples' lives," I continued, my voice rising.

"Don't forget," Griet said sourly, "you agreed to have Mack there."

She was right.

"Does that make me responsible for the shooting?"

Griet shrugged. "Of course not, dear. Who would have guessed?"

"I should have . . ."

"We're dealing with peoples' lives," she echoed me. "What do you think happens when your guests go off the air armed only with your sound byte therapy?"

I shrugged. "They go to the FRS clinic?"

"Some do. Most don't."

I was silent.

"Go home, Hanya. We have everything under control. When *Truth With Dr. H!* returns it will be bigger and better than ever."

"Because Dr. H is now the guest?"

"Perhaps."

"Okay, I'll go along with it. Just one request, Griet."

"Yes."

"Leave Sage out of this."

Griet stared at me, her eyes hard and unflinching. "It's a bit too late for that, Doctor. Don't you agree?"

3

Sage and I sat in Nom Wah, the oldest tea parlor in Chinatown Nearby, two bodyguards, hired by the network, watched. Robert and Isobel taped outside, following the storefronts down the narrow, crooked street. What were they shooting? Robert tried to follow us inside but I stopped him. Robert argued that he had the right to follow. He glanced at Sage. She nodded and he withdrew. I wondered if Robert had wired Sage and was taping everything for a voiceover.

I chose the noisy Chinatown restaurant for that reason. It would be difficult to hear anything and the location reminded me of Mack.

I'll probably get a reprimand from Griet.

I shrugged. This talk with Sage *had* to happen.

Nom Wah was located on Doyers Street, named after Dutchman Hendrick Doyer who purchased the property facing the Bowery in 1791. He ran a distillery. A century later, the street was nicknamed the *Bloody Angle* for the notorious Chinese Tong Gang killers who favored the location because of the sharp street angle and underground tunnels that connected the buildings. Hatchets were the choice of weapon, along with snickersnees – sword-like knives used as weapons. It all led to the expression "hatchet man." Herbert Asbury wrote about it in his 1928 book, *Gangs of New York:*

Armed with snickersnee and hatchet sharpened to a razor's edge, the tong killer lay in wait for his victim, and having cut him down as he came around the bend, fled . . . The police believe . . that more men have been murdered at the Bloody Angle than at any other place of like area in the world.

I imagined Mack dressed in black, slinking down the street, a hatchet in his hand and a *snickersee* in his belt. It wasn't pretty.

Sage waited for me to speak.

"He's using you," I began.

"Let's order."

"He's using you," I repeated.

She glanced through the window. Robert was giving Isobel instructions. Sage handed me one of the two plastic menus with photos of the small plate dishes. She held onto the paper sheet and pencil where we would circle our choices.

"My favorite is the salt & pepper spare ribs."

"Sage!"

"We have to get the sticky rice in lotus leaf and the Shanghainese Soup Dumplings. Best in the city."

I stared at her while she studied the menu.

"What else do you want?"

"Can't we talk?"

"I'm hungry. Let's order. Would you like some *char siu bao* – roast pork buns? Fried shrimp with bean curd skin or the rice rolls that you like so much?"

Sage circled the choices before I had a chance to respond.

Nom Wah was like an old friend. Espie and I had discovered the old tea parlor when we were kids. It was cheap – with red vinyl booths, yellow walls, and porcelain lucky cats. On the wall were autographed head shots of celebrities like Woody Allen and the beloved Chinese actor, Chow Yun-Fat. The waiters came around with pizza-sized metal serving trays filled with dishes of tasty-looking Chinese food. We didn't know what we ate. When we pointed to a dish that looked good, the waiter plopped it on the table. When we were full, the waiter counted up the plates and gave us a check in Chinese. It was all part of our adventure into mysterious Chinatown – more exotic to us than the old world Bronx Italian enclave on Arthur Avenue or *Yonah Schimmel's Knish Bakery,* a Jewish lower east side business established in 1890.

A few years ago, after numerous health department violations, the nephew of the owner, Wilson Tang, took over. Claiming a "reverse" career change for a Chinese-American, he reverted from a successful job in finance back to the restaurant business. He cleaned up the place, upgraded the kitchen, and resolved the violations. There were no more trays, just printed menus and check-off sheets like the one Sage held. The décor remained the same, only cleaner. Mismatched tea cups were still used and the old tea bar remained, with padded metal stools and cake stands filled with almond cookies.

The food was more delicious now than in the past. Some things *do* get better as they age.

Sage handed the sheet to the waiter and ordered two diet cokes.

I was silent.

The food arrived in random order.

"Why don't you talk to me," I said between bites of a luscious salt & pepper spare rib, very different from the standard sweet red ribs most Chinese restaurants served.

"Nothing to talk about."

"Nothing?"

Sage shrugged and peeled away a dark green lotus leaf to reveal sweet sticky rice.

"Stop." I touched her hand.

"This is the best . . ."

"Stop," I repeated. "We can't avoid this conversation."

Sage sighed and looked straight into my eyes.

I saw Espie's hazel eyes and wild red hair. Unconsciously, Sage patted the hamsa she always wore as if the damn thing would protect her.

I prayed silently that our talk would go well.

4

"Before you say anything," Sage took a bite of my favorite, salt & pepper spare ribs, "I have one question."

"What?"

"Did you see *Reddit*?"

"Reddit?"

"Of course – you probably don't know what I'm talking about." Sage reached for her iPhone and tapped the screen until she was satisfied. "Here."

It was on the hot list. Posted anonymously.

What's the real truth Dr. H?

Next to the post was a photo. I tapped it. The iPhone's screen filled with me staring at Mack in the audience, our eyes locked. Right before the shooting.

I gasped. "Who did this?"

Sage shrugged. "I saw it today. An hour ago. It'll go viral – they always do."

I shivered. "It looks like . . ."

Sage finished my sentence. "Like you were signaling Mack to shoot."

Suddenly the most delicious food in Chinatown tasted like ash. I couldn't speak.

"Do you think . . . ?"

Sage patted my hand. "Of course I don't think you're involved. Whoever posted on Reddit is going to continue . . . Twitter, Facebook, Instagram . . . you name it. Then there will be a video on YouTube. It's the way of the world. We're not invisible. The talk will go viral – you, Ayla, Moeda . . . *everyone.*"

My heart started to pound. I was breathless as I thought about the headlines.

Is Dr. H truthful?

Will the real shooter please rise?

Was it all a setup?

"Do I have enemies?" I whispered.

"Everyone has enemies. Celebrities have more enemies than most . . . people love to tell stories, make up conspiracy theories, spread rumors . . . I'm not telling you anything you don't know."

"It's so easy to do."

"Yes, Hanya, it's very easy. That's why I have to ask you this *before* you ask me anything."

I nodded.

"Did you have anything to do with this?"

I was shocked. "How can you think . . ?"

"That wasn't my question."

"Absolutely not," I sputtered. "Why would I want this kind of thing on my show?"

"Ratings," Sage said softly.

I glared at her.

Sage nodded. "Okay, let me ask you another way. Did you know that Mack would be in the audience?"

I didn't know what to say.

Sage waved a triangle of scallion pancake in the air. "Exactly what I thought."

5

I knew. Did I care?

I thought about how we scripted the show.

Ayla's ex-73 year old boyfriend, Mack will be in the audience. He was the father of Ayla's abandoned child. Ayla and Moeda are shocked as Mack rises from a strategically-placed seat in the center of the small audience. The audience boos and cries. Mack approaches the stage, sits down next to Dr. H, opposite the women, and sparks fly. Maybe someone calls in with information

about the abandoned child. Or maybe the child calls in and appears on a follow-up.

It sounded so right at the time.

"I knew," I whispered to Sage. "But I never thought he would have a gun. Or try to kill anyone. We have security to protect against that."

"It was a one-bullet *Liberator*," Sage said with disgust. She carefully placed an uneaten spare rib on the plate. "A homemade plastic gun doesn't get picked up by security."

"How could I know that?"

"It was all about the ratings. Isn't that what *media psychology* is about?"

I tried to object, find a way to erase the revulsion on Sage's face.

There was nothing to say. My tongue felt thick and furry. Truth is a strange concept. It can work both for and against you.

Sage nodded. "Who else? The production team. Griet? Visch? The warm-up crew?"

My hands trembled.

Sage snapped the spare rib with her teeth. I watched helplessly. There was no defense.

"I decided to do an investigation on my own – looking for Mack's accomplice," Sage continued. "I talked to Mallah, Remez, and Ayla. I even went to see Moeda but of course, she's in a coma. I discussed it with Steen. Nothing came out that I could see. Of course, I didn't know I was missing all those *other* people from the show. The list of possibilities just grew by a lot of names."

"You forgot one name," I said softly.

"Who?"

"Robert."

Sage's eyes flashed with anger.

"I know you're sleeping with him."

"So?"

"I don't trust him."

"You don't have to trust him."

"He's 20 years older than you."

"Twenty-three years to be exact."

"Why are you bothering with him?"

"Enough. It doesn't matter whether or not you like Robert. He's just taping this."

"The more stuff there is . . . the greater the notoriety . . . the more benefits he gets from you."

"Maybe so," Sage retorted, "but Robert is a latecomer to the scene. It's more likely to be someone who *knew* that Mack was coming and wanted . . . needed . . . the ratings to soar."

"Are you suggesting . . . ?"

"I'm not suggesting anything," Sage frowned. "I'm trying to figure out who helped Mack into the audience, why he sent the talcum powder that looked like ricin, and how he got into our apartment to kill the cat. You can say as much as you want about Robert – I know you don't like him, but Mack's buddy was on the scene long before Robert appeared."

I didn't want Sage to be right. I shuddered just thinking that it might be someone from the studio – a grand plan to boost ratings. Who? The most obvious suspect was the one person who had been dragging me along, disregarding my frustration.

Griet – like a red rose stuck in the snow.

6

After lunch, I hailed a cab and went to the studio. I knocked on Griet's office door, not waiting for permission to enter.

Griet admitted me into her post-modern wilderness.

"You knew."

"Knew what?" She smiled with her lips not her eyes.

"About Mack."

"We all knew he was in the audience, Hanya. So did you."

"Yes. None of us knew he had a gun."

"What are you trying to say?"

"You set this up. To increase ratings."

"Me?"

"Of course. Who else?"

"I think you're being dramatic, Hanya. Why would I set up a shooting? After all, I wouldn't know *how* to buy a gun, much less make a homemade one."

"You could figure it out."

"It's a nice story, a shame that it's not true."

"It *is* true. Sage said . . ."

"What did your precious niece say? She knows as much about TV as the man she's sleeping with."

"Don't talk about her like that."

Griet laughed. There was pure spite in her eyes. "Well isn't she, Hanya? Sleeping with The Senator's Son?"

"What does that have to do with . . .?"

"It doesn't, my dear. It has as little to do with the shooting as your outrageous niece claims. We run an honest show about real people. We offer help – free help from the Family Reigns Supreme Mental Health Clinic. We don't shoot people; we educate them, showing the viewing audience problems they identify with, and how to solve them effectively. It's the *truth*. We're very important media psychologists. All of us. Even you. We serve a critical role in the community."

The community? What community?

My boss sounded like a commercial.

"What are you saying, Griet? Are you denying . . ?"

Griet looked past me. "How did that sound?"

What was she talking about? I turned around, trying to get a handle on what was happening. Robert was standing behind me, a grin on his face, while Isobel taped everything.

"Did you get that Robert?" Griet said pleasantly.

"It's a wrap," Robert responded smoothly. "Particularly the bit about Dr. H's niece sleeping with The Senator's Son. Nice touch."

I was too horrified to speak.

7

It was predictable. My conversation with Griet morphed into a You Tube video.

Sage was appalled. "How could you . . ." she sputtered.

"How could I? That was your . . . boyfriend taping the whole thing."

"He didn't say the words."

"I didn't either. It was Griet."

"It doesn't matter. They were said . . ."

"And Robert was thrilled. *He* posted the video."

Sage was silent, struggling to compose herself.

"That's what your lover thinks of you. A celebrity byte. The Senator's Son with The Infamous Media Psychologist's niece. Great stuff."

Sage's face fell, as if she had been hit. I had seen it before. "I'm sorry," I said softly. "You trusted the wrong man. Again."

My phone buzzed with a new text.

Did u see it on You Tube?

Tamirah. She never missed a beat.

Yes

Is it true?

Yes

OK. We'll make the best of it.

Ignore it.

It's going viral.

I know.

I shook my head. Tamirah was always on top of things.

Sage saw me studying my cell phone. "Are you okay?"

"Of course."

"You don't look okay."

I handed her the phone. "Did you see this?"

"Yes."

"Sage, what are you thinking?"

"Nothing. I'm just having a good time."

"Are you?"

Sage lowered her eyes. "Of course I am. That's why I do it. Maybe you should try some sex for a change. It eases stress . . ."

"Sage!"

She shrugged. "Just a thought."

Just a thought. It was crazy. I had no shows, patients, answers, and only Ayla to keep me company. However, maybe the kids had the right idea. Do what you want and think about it *after*. Years brought reluctance – hesitation. I needed something more exciting in my life. Why should 66 years stop me?

"Live," Sage said softly. "Isn't that what it's all about? Live and feel good and take risks. So I'm on You Tube. Who cares? I'm doing The Senator's Son. Who cares? I'm living, Hanya, don't you see?"

I did see.

I felt like a city flower, blooming in an impossible place.

8

It was time to take control – listen to Sage and figure out what was happening. I felt like a sleuth from a mystery novel, plotting my investigation. Watch out Steen. I was on my way.

I had to move quickly, ask questions, and take action. *Live*, like Sage advised. There was nothing to stop me. I began with the obvious. Who were all the people that surrounded me, claimed loyalty, and turned quickly? Robert, Griet, Visch, even Sage. Were they suspects? Or did they believe *I* was the culprit? The only one

I could ask was Moeda and she was in a coma. The more time she spent unconscious, the less likely she was to come out of it – at least, come out of it *intact*. The answers dangled like the sword of Damocles, ready to slice off my head.

I had to cut off some heads before that happened. *That* was exciting. *That* was living.

I made a plan.

If I dressed in nondescript clothes, messed my hair, and went without makeup, no one would recognize me. I could slip through crowds unnoticed. My celebrity would be buried with my accoutrements in a prince-and-the-pauper scenario.

Who would notice a plain, poorly-dressed, 66 year old woman, determined to find answers? An old lady looking for an old killer ducking the digital eyes of the son of an even older man, The Senator?

I loved the scenario. There was poetry in age deceiving youth; wisdom conquering beauty; and a cultural blindness of people who rarely looked at a face over 50 unless it was made for TV.

I savored the anonymity.

Take that Detective Steen.

There had to be a book in this. Perhaps a best-seller called *Truth With Dr. H!: The Real Story*. I could see it now – hardcover, paperback, ebook, articles, blogs, book tours, on and offline – the potential was enormous. I calculated the stats – there were 78 million potential baby boomer readers who would belong to me.

How's that for ratings, Griet?

Disguised as an old lady fumbling with electronics, I purchased a mini tablet with a fine point stylus to keep notes. I paid for it in cash; I wanted no paper or digital trail. I hid it in a cheap tote bag that I bought on the street for ten bucks, paired with dirty white sneakers.

Drooping a grey streak across my forehead, I let my roots edge to the surface. Searching the discount clothing stores, I purchased navy polyester pants and several print blouses that tucked in, exaggerating my middle. I didn't wear a belt or expensive jewelry. I added a pair of smudged, shaky sunglasses. When I put the pieces together, I disappeared. Who would imagine that I was anything but a grandma shopping in the city for sales?

I felt like a cheap, aging combo between Patterson's Alex Cross and Women's Murder Club. Play the part, I giggled. Who can do it better than Dr. H? I could follow anyone, anywhere.

No one would know.

I was invisible.

9

I began with Ayla.

I figured she would be the easiest. Since I knew where Sage went for her steamy rendezvous with Robert, I already had some answers. I was afraid to track Griet or Visch, assuming they would be careful about their movements. It required more experience, which I would develop as my investigation progressed. Moeda was useless and Mallah and Remez would probably lead me into city neighborhoods where I would be recognized. There was always Robert, but I knew the man was too dangerous *and* Sage would be furious.

I didn't have to worry about Tamirah.

I was doing something exciting, like Sage suggested. I felt alive, never imagining that it could turn deadly serious. Ayla left the apartment, thinking I was taking a nap. I waited a few minutes, put on my disguise, and rode the elevator down to Remez.

"Which way did she go?" I asked the doorman.

Remez gave me a strange look. His eyes moved from my dirty white sneakers, to the cheap tote bag, and rested on the cheap crumpled print blouse. He wanted to say something but resisted.

"She forgot her tablet." I waved my mini. "She hates going anywhere without it."

Remez nodded. He pointed to *The Dubliner*, a replica Irish pub built on land probably once owned by a famous New Amsterdam Jew, Asser Levy. I followed but didn't see her stringy, caramel-colored hair until she turned right onto Broad Street. I knew where she was headed. I slipped between pedestrians as she made a left onto Beaver Street. She paused, looked at the tourist-shrouded charging bull, and then walked alongside the black iron fence of *Bowling Green Park*.

She entered the Bowling Green Subway Station, across from *The National Museum of the American Indian,* housed in the old *Alexander Hamilton U.S. Custom House*. My world was filled with history.

I followed her to the #5 uptown, staying as far away as possible. I was pretty good at this spy stuff. Ayla looked around as she waited for the train. For a moment I thought she saw me, but I dodged behind a group of noisy tourists. There was no sign of recognition.

A #5 train arrived and Ayla stepped into the car. I took the one that followed. I leaned against the door between cars and watched as Ayla found a seat, flanked by a grungy kid with earphones, carrying books, and an Asian man dressed in an inexpensive grey business suit.

I waited.

Twenty minutes later we arrived at Grand Central Station. Ayla transferred to the #6. Both lines were originally owned by the Interborough Rapid Transit Company, or IRT, and purchased by the city in 1940.

The ride lasted for over 40 minutes. People came and went; a blur of faces that were interesting, sad, reflecting every emotion and lifestyle in New York. It struck me that the New York Subway System was a great equalizer – millionaires sat next to homeless, never acknowledging one another. Every race, religion, and ethnicity came and went, oblivious of one another. The girl in torn jeans could come from the wealthy Upper East Side; the man in khakis might live in the south Bronx. The dark-skinned man was probably Pakistani; the black-hatted Hassid sat next to a Muslim woman in a *Habib*. People didn't care unless their space was invaded and the unwritten subway rules broken. Even during rush hour, when people were pressed up against one another, eyes glazed to protect against the invasion of body space.

A street performer sat in my car, strumming on his guitar, his eyes in a place beyond the New York Subway. He sang a Ladino song in a soothing tenor.

Where is the key that was in the drawer?
My forefathers brought it with great pain
From their house in Spain.

We told our children this is the heart of our home.

I dropped a one dollar bill in his cup as he stood up and worked the car. He smiled and thanked me. At 86th Street he left and went into Ayla's car. She glanced at him and turned away, her eyes focused on the small strip, suspended from the ceiling, which announced each stop.

We crossed beneath the Harlem River and into the Bronx. The names and areas were vaguely familiar, memories from my childhood in East Tremont. I shivered. It was an odd coincidence that Ayla was headed in this direction. Suddenly I was scared. Where *was* she taking me? Did she sense I was following her? Was she leading me into a trap?

My heart raced. Why was I riding into the past? I hadn't belonged in this world since the 1950s. Maybe I should turn around, go home, and give up this tawdry mystery act? Let the professionals like Steen figure it out.

I thought of Sage, Griet, Robert, Visch, and all the other people who had reason to back Mack, agitate my *show,* and shoot Moeda. I was curious, rebellious, looking for adventure and inadvertently challenged by Sage. There was no turning back.

Right before Whitlock Avenue, the subway changed into an elevated track. Streets whizzed by below, building tops next to us – it was a mosaic of outer borough life.

Suddenly, Ayla stood. I glanced at the sign. *East Tremont Avenue.*

I could hardly breathe. Images of Espie, Mother, Father and the old neighborhood filled my mind. The old community was long gone, thank you Robert Moses. So why did it make my heart pound and my palms sweat? What secret memories had I repressed – memories that were suddenly ignited by being on the long forgotten street? Old images flickered through my head.

. . . a brick tenement turned grey after a half-century of city pollution. The front had a metal fire escape that zigzagged down five stories. A concrete stoop led to the entrance; steps served as meeting ground, playground, and shared space. The street was narrow – few people owned cars and kids could play punch ball and stick ball marking off bases with chalk and sewer covers. Vendors called out wares and services, from pickles and used clothing to knife sharpening. Mothers bent their heads and shared gossip; fathers argued politics.

I shook my head angrily. It wasn't the time for the voices of my childhood. I forced myself back to the present. I had almost lost Ayla. I scanned the station and saw her descending the steps to the street. Taking a deep breath, I followed. Dizzy with recall, I descended the first set of steps, and went through a large space with more steps and a famous stained glass triptych by Romare Barden. The bright colors reflected a busy city scene.

Ayla left the station and made her way through an arched tunnel over the sidewalk. A fruit and vegetable seller watched her, hoping she would buy something. Ayla ignored him and made her way down Westchester Avenue, going left on East Tremont Avenue. She paused at the East Tremont, Fink, and Westchester Avenue sign.

Smiling, she retraced her steps and entered Westchester Square Park. The park held the Owen Dolan Recreation and Golden Age Center, overlooking a large sandy area with benches and a lot of pigeons. I raced back to the arched tunnel, hoping I could hide in the shadows and watch her without being seen.

At the near end of the park was a strange sculpture – a large, federal-style bronze chair mounted on a granite boulder. The boulder had line drawings of wild boars playing, fighting, and feeding their young. Under the seat was a bronze Merriam Webster Dictionary. David Saunders, the artist, described it as a "seat of honor."

It was one of the oddest sculptures I had ever seen.

No charging bull or George Washington.

It was just a chair. A few yards away was an old man standing with his back to me.

Across the park, I saw Ayla headed for the seat of honor. Why? She was smiling at the old man. I took a few steps outside the tunnel. She never saw me – her eyes were fixed on the man. Ayla took a few more steps then leaped into his arms. They embraced hungrily. Ayla clung to him like a teenager. He stroked her hair tenderly. They kissed and separated. They stepped apart, held hands, and kissed again. He put one arm around her and began to walk toward me.

I broke into a sweat.

I fled through the tunnel and up the stairs, stumbling and praying they hadn't seen me. I jumped on the first train going downtown. I was the only one in the car. I checked the stairs through the dirty window. They hadn't followed.

I always hated the Bronx. I was glad to leave, unlike Espie and Mother. Father and I agreed on *that*. Yet I couldn't get the image out of my mind.

Two people embracing in front of the seat of honor.

Ayla.

And Mack.

10

My next stop was the hospital.

Moeda had been moved out of ICU to a private room, compliments of Griet and the network. She lay in her bed, crisp white sheets tucked neatly around her, various monitors, drips, and equipment hooked to her body. I stared at her for a long time.

"I wish you could talk," I said finally.

Moeda didn't respond.

"What would you tell me? Ayla and Mack never broke up? You never really trusted Ayla? Ayla and Mack were lovers and had set up this entire scenario?"

Her eyelids fluttered.

"Are you waking up, Moeda?" I asked excitedly.

"No," the nurse said from behind me. "It's an automatic response."

"To what I'm saying?"

The nurse shrugged. "Who knows?" The nurse left and I returned to Moeda. "Maybe you know nothing," I said gently. "I hope you eventually wake up, return to life . . . tell us."

A single tear made its way down my cheek. I wiped it away angrily. "I have to be strong for you, and for everyone else until we figure this out."

Moeda didn't move.

11

I left Moeda's room.

Detective Steen was waiting for me.

"What are you doing here?" I tried to cover my surprise.

His face was unreadable. "Following leads."

"Following me?"

"Why would I follow you?"

"You shouldn't."

Steen sighed. "Of course I shouldn't." He touched my arm and led me into an empty waiting room.

We faced off.

"Why did you visit Moeda?"

"Why did *you*?"

"Why are you dressed like . . ." he paused trying to find the words.

I had forgotten about my disguise. I laughed, oddly pleased that he noticed. "I didn't want anyone to recognize me."

"Why?"

"Questions," I lied. "Everyone has questions for Dr. H."

"Where were you going?"

"Nowhere." I corrected myself. "Rather, I was going home after the hospital."

Steen stepped back and examined my face and clothes, running his eyes over my entire body.

"Going home?"

"Yes." My voice shook.

He smiled tightly and ran the tip of his tongue over his bottom lip. "You need to be careful, Hanya. Maybe fans don't recognize you but it's harder to hide from your enemies."

"I don't have enemies."

He laughed. "Everyone has enemies, my dear."

I shrugged. "Are you finished?"

"No. Not quite."

"What else do you want to know?"

"What you know."

"I don't understand."

He stepped closer until his face was inches from mine. "I have this feeling that you know more than you're telling, Doctor. I can smell it."

I allowed him to linger. It was odd, but I *liked* his closeness, as if something very old was stirred up inside. Sage would have been pleased. Reluctantly, I stepped back. "No secrets," I said softly.

"There are a lot of secrets," he chided me. "Some we know – others we have yet to reveal. In the end, they all surface. If it's inside, it's destined to come out."

"I don't believe that."

"Eh?"

"People keep secrets if they want to shield themselves from . . . eyes like you have."

"Eyes that see more than most?"

"Maybe."

"You know," Steen stepped closer, backing me against the wall. "My eyes see a lot."

"Really? What do you see?" I laughed nervously.

He reached across the space and touched my cheek with the tip of his finger. I held my breath, unable to move.

Suddenly a couple entered the waiting room. Their faces were sad; clothes disheveled; they clutched a pile of small photo albums. Steen backed away. I had this inexplicable feeling that something had been lost – a moment in time interrupted by a world that refused to leave us alone.

"Another time," Steen whispered.

He left. I watched his back as he headed toward Moeda's room. Should I follow? Should I run? Another time?

What the hell just happened?

12

The next day I took Sage for another meal at *Nom Wah*. I wore my normal clothes, hiding my disguise at the back of my closet.

Robert wasn't following us. Where was he? Did it matter? I knew the answers but didn't know what to do with the information.

We ordered the white dough roast pork bun. Sage chose Shanghainese soup dumplings.

I selected a Nom Wah special, shrimp and snowpea leaf dumplings.

Sage happily plunged into the food.

I didn't move.

"What's the matter?" Sage paused; a Shanghainese soup dumpling nestled in her spoon.

"I have to tell you something."

She popped the dumpling into her mouth and reached for another. "It's not about Robert again?"

"No. It's not about Robert."

"Why aren't you eating?"

I picked up a spare rib. "Is that better?"

"Yes." Sage selected a pork bun. "Now talk."

"I followed Ayla."

"What?"

"I followed Ayla to see if I could figure things out."

"That doesn't make sense."

I shrugged.

"Why do you have to follow anyone? Do you follow me as well?"

"You know better than that."

"Then why?"

"I wanted to investigate – help Steen."

"Are you moving from tabloid to crime drama?" Sage chuckled. "Do we have another Miss Marple here?" She grinned at her reference to Agatha Christie's classic spinster sleuth.

I frowned. "This is serious."

Sage's eyes twinkled. "And what, my dear, did you find? A murder at the vicarage or a body in the library?"

"Stop it. I might not be young but I'm not dead."

"Sorry."

"I found . . . discovered, something we should all know. I just don't know what to do with it."

"What truth did you find, Dr. H?"

I ignored her sarcasm.

"Ayla."

"You said that already."

"Ayla *and Mack*."

Sage froze.

"What did you say?"

"Ayla and Mack."

"Together?"

"Together."

"I don't understand."

I told Sage how I followed Ayla into the Bronx and East Tremont.

"They were embracing . . . kissing."

"How do you know it was Mack?"

"How many seventy-three year old men featured on YouTube kiss younger women?"

"More than you think."

I sighed. "I *know* his face – I saw it over and over on Reddit, YouTube, Facebook . . ."

"Okay, I get it."

"It was really them, Sage. *Together.*"

"Why would Ayla be with Mack? He tried to kill her mother."

I took a small bite of a spare rib. The crunchy, salty flavor filled my mouth. I savored the moment. Slowly, I swallowed and reached for my diet soda. Sage watched me, mesmerized. I let the instant hold, like a minute of silence in the middle of media frenzy.

"That," I said finally, "is exactly what I want to know."

13

Sage and I went in different directions after we left *Nom Wah.*

We had no answers, only vague suspicions that included each other as suspects. I had to think things through – was I a bigger part of this than I wanted to admit? Did I subconsciously want the shooting, the infamy, and the ratings?

Sage headed uptown, probably to Robert. I wondered what it was like making love with the narcissistic middle-aged man. Did he touch her in the right places? Did he force her to act out his fantasies? Did he revel in her youth?

I shivered. I had dealt with the mundane and fantastical sexual proclivities of patients for my entire professional life. It was painful to visualize what Robert might be doing to Sage. I had heard stories about his father and assumed that the son could share similar sexual appetites. I didn't trust father or son and was afraid Robert would hurt Sage. At the same time, I didn't think that Robert was Mack's accomplice.

Inexplicably, I was drawn to the cemetery at St. James Place.

It was the burial ground of the Sephardic Jews in New Amsterdam. Originally much larger, only a small remnant remained. Most of the bodies had been removed by the city in 1855. I walked down St. James Place and peered through the thick, iron fence that was mounted on a stone wall enclosing the graveyard. Towering buildings surrounded the old burial ground, their walls scarred and dirty; dull windows overlooked the tiny time-stamp. There were a few trees, flowers, and bushes that struggled to guard the space. I ran my hand along the cold black iron fence. The cemetery was chained shut – no one could enter without permission from The Spanish and Portuguese Synagogue now located at Central Park West at 70th Street.

I read the plaque as I had many times before.

It was a strange, forgotten place, silent in the city noise. I peered between the bars. A few yellow flowers struggled to survive between the tombstones. An odd sadness filled me.

Sounds were muted as if I had stepped back in time. Someone or something spoke to me from the old graves. I knew that several relatives were buried there – my ancestors from Recife, Brazil who had won sanctuary in Dutch New Amsterdam. Most graves were lost, but the ones that remained with thin, uneven stones that looked about to topple or a few above-ground mausoleums, were markers of lives that couldn't be denied. A century later, after establishing themselves in the New World, my ancestors were fierce supporters of George Washington. On the night of *Yom Kippur*, when Jews were praying on the most religious holiday of the year, George Washington arrived in Newport, his troops cold and starving, requesting help. The Jews left their Shul to save the men.

Moses Seixas, the leader of the Newport Jewish community, later wrote to Washington on behalf of his Congregation.

. . . the children of the Stock of Abraham ask God to send the Angel who conducted our forefathers through the wilderness into the Promised Land [to] conduct you through all the difficulties and dangers of this mortal life.

George Washington guaranteed religious freedom, permanently ensuring the right of Jews to live in the United States.

What did a TV tabloid show *mean* in comparison to them?

Words echoed in my head, along with Mother's voice, telling us about people we never met but were a part of our blood. People whose remains lay before me in this tiny spot of land. Among all the stories, I felt a powerful kinship with one woman, Chana DePiza, whose remains lay deep within these grounds.

"Chana," I whispered. "I don't have your strength. Tell me what to do."

I waited for an answer. What to do? Where to go? How do I understand the strange list of characters in front of me? I stared at Chana's headstone, carved with a delicate flower.

The smell of flowers seemed to fill the air. A gentle voice echoed in my mind. Chana? Genetic memories? A good imagination? I didn't know the answer. It felt as though she was telling me how to interpret my life.

It's what we were destined to do – what God wants. Go and live well.

Go and live well? What did that mean? Better ratings? Exposing Ayla? Leaving Sage to her self-destructive behavior and supporting her when she fell?

I waited for another message. There was nothing. Slowly the mute lifted; I was back into a world of honking cars, snorting trucks, people rushing, the city world moving at a furious pace. Chana had given me a message but I had no idea what she meant. *Go and live well.*

I took a deep breath and headed home.

14

Steen was waiting for me at Munsee Court. He chatted with Remez as I walked down the street. It was strange. The Detective waiting for *me*? Remez was silent as Steen greeted me.

"I was wondering," he smiled, "if I could talk to you."

I looked at the stocky, powerfully built cop, ten years younger than me.

It's what we were destined to do – what God wants. Go and live well.

I shook the words from my head and nodded. "Of course. Here or upstairs?"

"Just a few questions. Upstairs would be fine."

We took the elevator to my apartment, maintaining appropriate personal space.

"It's a beautiful day. Would you like to talk on the terrace?"

"Of course. If you're comfortable."

I led The Detective through the foyer, past the country kitchen table and into the living room. I opened the sliding glass doors and stepped out. He followed.

I closed the doors behind us and glanced up at the dense buildings. Steen was silent. He scanned the 50 feet of outdoor space, his eye pausing at the terra cotta tiles and clear railings. He walked toward the wrought iron table that stood in front of the copy of the statue of Peter Stuyvesant. The Detective sighed as if preparing for an interrogation.

"Are you a fan of Peter Stuyvesant?"

"Yes, very much. I always imagined us having like minds. He was a great man determined to hold onto New Amsterdam for his fatherland."

"He didn't succeed."

"I know. He did his best, though. The Director-General had many failings but hard work and loyalty wasn't among them."

I didn't respond.

The Detective stared at the surrounding city.

"This is quite a terrace."

"Yes. It convinced me that I had to own this place."

"You're fortunate. I live in a much simpler space."

I shrugged.

"Midtown," he added. "With my boy, Claus."

"No other children?"

"My wife and I are divorced. My daughter Jan lives with her."

I nodded.

"Please, sit down."

The Detective glanced at Peter Stuyvesant then sat in one of the padded chairs. I joined him, several feet away. Instead of facing each other, we looked out, between the buildings, to the water. We didn't speak for several minutes.

"You had to talk to me?" I asked softly. "Ask more questions?"

Our eyes met. He gazed at me in a visual embrace. Was I getting the correct message from The Detective?

Steen took a deep breath. "I'm concerned about you," he said finally.

"Professionally?"

He gave me a strange look. "Of course."

"Then you don't have to be. I'm fine."

"We all have it, you know." He studied my face.

"Have what?"

His voice changed. "The evil within."

"You mean the potential to be a psychopath?"

"Yes."

"Of course. I'm a clinical psychologist – I know about such things."

He nodded. "What makes us different is that we control it – stop it. We insulate ourselves in heavy coats of morals and pretend it doesn't exist."

"Like wolves and humans," I mumbled.

"What?"

"Nothing."

He shrugged. "We agree that the predator – the psychopath – only pretends to be *human?*"

"I've dealt with many psychopaths. On and off TV. Some murder, others destroy in different ways. They don't care. What point are you trying to make?"

"Okay, Doctor, I'll be more direct."

"Thank you."

"Mack is a psychopath. We all know that. What we need to find out is the identity of his *accomplice*. Who had the idea to shoot Moeda? Kill Mirasol? Was it Mack or the accomplice's idea to use the Internet? If it was the accomplice's idea, then he or she is *younger* than Mack."

"Are you saying that older people can't use the Internet?"

"No. I'm saying that older people are less likely to use the Internet as a weapon."

Good comeback.

The Detective weighed his words. "Have you ever heard of *gilgul*?"

"Of course. The Kabbalistic belief in the recycling of souls."

"Yes."

He waited. For what? I didn't speak. Our eyes locked.

"Do you feel it?"

"Do I feel *what*?" I struggled to contain my instincts. Yet it hit me so hard that the buildings began to swirl, the terrace blurred . . . I caught my breath. There was a face, although I couldn't make it out. Fisted hands. Ragged breath drunk with our pain. I struggled to see beyond the glistening eyes.

A bear licking his paws after a kill.

A wolf stalking his prey.

A vulture swooping from the sky, joyous over the capture of a doomed and terrified rodent trapped in its talons.

A voice.

"You see it. The way I see it?"

The Detective.

Slowly, I returned to the present.

"You have the sense?" The Detective said slowly. He took a deep breath; his huge chest expanded with the effort.

"What? What do you want me to see?"

Steen's blue eyes captured mine. "I don't understand it. I know it's a connect between us as if we knew each other *before*."

"Before what?"

"Another life."

"I don't believe in reincarnation."

"You don't have to believe in reincarnation or *gilgul*. Just feel it."

"Are you kidding?"

"I wish I was. I wish I didn't have this *thing* . . . like a vulture who senses carrion before he sees it." He shook his head. "I see it in you and that's why I'm here."

I laughed. "You believe I have *that*?"

Me? The voice of truth?

"I know it."

"How?"

He touched his chest. "Here, in my heart. I know you have it . . . I know we've shared this before, but now I'm afraid it will get you in trouble. I don't want you to get hurt."

Ayla. Mack.

"I'm already hurt."

The Detective leaned closer and took my hand. His fingers curled around mine and electric shocks traveled through my hand and up my arm. I tried to speak but no words came.

"Don't fight it, Hanya."

I pulled my hand away.

"This is ridiculous. You sound like a teenager."

He smiled sadly. "I'll accept that for the moment. Eventually, you'll *see*. You won't need me to show you. Don't be afraid – our connect goes beyond today, to another time . . ."

I stood up. "Thank you," I said stiffly. "If I have any more questions, I'll contact you."

"Of course, doctor. I'll find my way out, but I'll be back."

He left.

15

I stared at the buildings, peered at the water, and studied the statue of Peter Stuyvesant. What did it mean? What did Mack and Ayla have and why was I suddenly a part of their story? Was it the show? Did it have anything to do with Griet's ruthless craving for ratings or her soberly protective Jake Visch? Where did Sage and Robert fit in? How did a crazy New Age cop get the case?

Why was Mirasol so brutally murdered?

Tears sprang to my eyes.

A sweet voice entered my head – a voice I hadn't heard since childhood. It was Espie.

"I believe in gilgul," Espie said secretively.

"What's gilgul?" I asked.

"The recycling of souls."

"I don't get it."

"Gilgul neshamot – the cycling of souls."

"Hebrew?"

"Yes."

"I don't speak Hebrew."

"It doesn't matter. Let me tell you the secret.

"I love secrets."

"The Early Kabbalists said that every soul is destined to return to heaven. If a soul hasn't worked things out on Earth, it can assume a new body and come back."

"I still don't get it."

Espie hugged me. "Don't worry, Hanya, some day you will."

Was that day here? Is that what Steen was trying to tell me?

I don't know exactly why I did it. Something told me to rush into my bedroom and change into my favorite *Roberto Cavalli* jeans. They made me feel better – almost young and sexy. I giggled and headed back to the terrace.

Steen stood there, next to the statue of Peter Stuyvesant.

"I thought you left."

He looked at my jeans, then my face. I blushed.

He was silent. My eyes locked with The Detective. I don't know why I did it. I didn't plan to do it, but there was something pounding in my head that I couldn't stop. I moved as if otherworldly forces controlled me.

It's what we were destined to do. Go and live well.

I fell into his arms.

16

My world shuddered.

I didn't believe in reincarnation, karma, and spirits – any of those things. I was a scientist; a psychologist who *knew* that we were born, lived our lives, and then died. The end. Nothing after.

Now Espie was talking to me.

A psychopath and his accomplice were stalking me.

And The Detective was kissing me.

It made no sense. Wasn't I too old for a philosophical revision? I lived by clearly organized truths. All these people and events were conspiring to tell me that there was another truth that I hadn't incorporated into my personal paradigm. Was it possible? Did it make everything else a lie – a fantasy – an illusion of fame and productivity?

The Detective was the key. Why had I responded like a kid? *Like Sage?* I was too old for that stuff. A voice inside me laughed. I was the last red leaf in autumn . . . determined to stay alive.

Age had nothing to do with it.

Sage
and
Robert

1

I couldn't believe my eyes.

I shook my head and blinked. Was this for real? Or was it a movie with a bad scene, an outtake that was bizarre and funny at the same time?

I was supposed to be with Robert. I was getting tired – perhaps leery – of his games. He took me too far into his odd fantasies. They were *his,* not mine. I told him I needed to work on my dissertation. It wasn't a lie – designing, researching, and writing a dissertation was a consuming job. The completion and publication of my work would leave me at the top of a new and burgeoning field – *predicting future violence in young children.* It sounded like an odd choice but given my past, was plausible.

I left the library early, my laptop filled with new research and links. Maybe I would ask Hanya for dinner? She was restless since the suspension of her show. Her once large practice had dwindled – most people didn't feel safe confiding in a celebrity unless it was on national TV. I smirked. Imagine Robert telling *his* stories? The Senator would go nuts; social media would leap on it like stray dogs; and the "press" would splash it across the front pages of TV, radio, internet, You Tube, Twitter, and Facebook . . .

I shook my head. How did we all get here?

Robert could make Representative Anthony Weiner's dick displayed on Twitter look boring.

Maybe I should tape Robert?

The thought was even funnier. Expose The Senator and his Son? Add them to the ongoing lists of sex scandals, bedrooms online, and Twitter-style gossip that everyone devoured like hogs on a rampage. I would never expose Hanya in that way. Yet Hanya understood the trade-off of media therapy for psychotherapy. Play with celebrity and you risk the hazards of publicity. Hanya remained clean until now. The peril entered her studio, on the tailwinds of a scandal-never-exposed, dug up from the graveyard of human behavior that cloned itself, over and over. Hanya had her choices. Ayla and Moeda were *invited* to her show. She knew Mack was going to be in the audience. Now, Hanya was questioning her decisions. Why else did she follow Ayla and make pointless trips to strategize with Griet and Jake Visch?

A good dinner – and talk – might help.

Crossing Bowling Green, I saw Ayla entering the subway. Maybe she was meeting Mack? Hanya and I didn't know what to do with the information so we kept quiet, agreeing not to tell Steen. Who knew where *he* would take it?

I glanced at the park. It was New York City's oldest. The spot once served as council ground for Native American tribes and later, the Dutch called it the "Plain." It was the beginning of High Street (now Broadway) – a trade route that had run north through Manhattan and the Bronx. Bowling Green was used for parades, a meeting place, and a cattle market.

I turned and looked south of Bowling Green to the old Alexander Hamilton U.S. Customs House, built on the original site of 17th century Fort Amsterdam. The Fort had once been the soul of New Amsterdam. The Customs House was an elegant Beaux Arts structure that faced uptown rather than the water – a tribute to the city's extraordinary past. My eyes skimmed over the exterior sculptures of artist Daniel Chester French, an American best known for his statue of Abraham Lincoln in Washington D.C.'s Lincoln Memorial. I paused at two marble figures, part of a group known as "Seafaring Nations." Holland was on the left, flanked by Portugal. I felt an odd affinity to these stone men, as if I had known them in the flesh at one point in time.

Was that what Hanya meant when she spoke about our Sephardic legacy?

I shook my head impatiently. I didn't have the time to dwell on phantoms from the past when there were so many immediate concerns.

Yet the statues haunted me.

I turned away and walked the few short blocks to South William Street. I entered Munsee Court and Remez looked at me strangely. He was about to say something, then changed his mind. He nodded and looked away. I paused, giving him the opportunity to speak. Remez stared at the street.

I rode the elevator and entered the apartment. It was oddly quiet. I carefully placed my laptop and *Ferragamo Crossbody* satchel on the table in the foyer. The apartment was never noisy, except for Mallah's vacuum cleaner, but this was different. There was stillness as if unseen eyes were watching and waiting. I took a deep breath. Did something happen? An image of Mirasol and Hanya popped into my head. I had tried to convince Hanya to get a new cat but she resisted.

"I won't risk the life of another pet," she said. "No discussion."

Just like Hanya, making up her mind without considering the alternative. The woman could be stubborn; different from Grandma Espie.

I called out Hanya's name. No answer.

My skin crawled.

I inched my way across the foyer like a predator. Something was happening and I wasn't sure I needed to discover yet another truth.

I paused at the country kitchen table and took a deep breath. Something told me to slow down, grab a truffle, make a cup of tea, do anything but continue.

I put a dark chocolate lemon truffle in my mouth and waited for something to happen. Nothing. I took a dark chocolate Irish Cream next.

Still nothing. I peered into the living room. It was empty. I recalled the day when Robert arrived with his box of *La Maison Du Chocolat*. It was the first time I felt his heat. I sensed that something would happen between us. Then the doorman buzzed and the envelope was delivered with white powder. Ricin? Anthrax? I smiled bitterly over our raw fear. No one cared when we had to strip. We were terrified but Robert had time to examine my nudity.

Why wasn't he afraid?

It was so convenient how everything played out. Shooting. Texts. Ricin scare. Killing the cat. Robert.

Convenient for whom?

Moving past the couch, I headed toward the sliding glass doors. Maybe Hanya was on the terrace – she loved outdoor space.

"I can feel the energy of the city," she always said, "without walking the streets."

The strange statue of Peter Stuyvesant made me laugh. I thought of Hanya's words.

He stands there with his peg-leg, haughty and uncompromising. Perhaps the way he looked when our ancestors came from Recife, Brazil. I keep him here to remind me – remember – that Jews had to fight to live on this very street.

I grinned. Hanya still had the fight in her.

I slid open the glass door and called her name.

That's when I saw them.

2

Hanya and Steen were locked in one another's arms, kissing and holding hands.

I gasped. Too loud.

Hanya and The Detective? They were too damn old for *that*. They looked like a bunch of teenagers hooking up behind the school playground.

They heard me and parted quickly, smoothing their clothes and their dignity. Steen always looked wrinkled, so there wasn't much to hide. Hanya wore her favorite *Roberto Cavalli* jeans. That was the giveaway. Hanya only wore her *Cavalli's* on special occasions.

Only *I* would know that.

Their faces were flushed, their eyes a bit glazed.

"Hi . . . I thought I would come home early," I stammered.

They stared at me.

"You're supposed to be at the library," Hanya managed.

"I came home early. I thought we might have dinner."

Steen and Hanya watched me, red-faced. I couldn't help it. I stood there and laughed.

3

They tried to explain themselves.

I laughed harder.

They glared at me.

"Why do you think it's so funny for people our age to . . ." Hanya paused, searching for the right word.

Steen and I looked at her. We thought the same thing.

Why do you think it's so funny for people our age to do it?

That made me laugh more.

"Why do you think it's so funny for people our age to be . . . intimate." Hanya tried again.

Steen couldn't contain himself. He laughed with me, shaking his head. Initially, Hanya was angry. She looked at him and then at me. "Caught," she said lamely and joined the joke.

We remained like that for several minutes. I pulled over a chair and sat opposite them.

"I guess you were . . . working?" I giggled.

"We were . . ."

That started me laughing again.

"Enough," Hanya ordered. "You found us. Just don't tell anyone."

"Police policy," Steen added weakly.

"Of course."

"Listen, Sage. We might be old but we're not *dead*."

"Speak for yourself, ladies. I'm not old."

Hanya and I looked at Steen. Yeah, he was kind of good-looking in a very primal masculine way. Dark where Robert was light; thick where Robert was wiry. Too hairy for my tastes. Robert was smooth . . . maybe too smooth. He probably waxed his chest. Steen's piercing blue eyes were his finest feature. He fixed them on me.

He's not that much older than Robert.

It was an interesting thought – yet the two men were from very different worlds. Steen was law and order. Robert was creativity, experimentation, and the child of celebrity. It was hard to equate them.

"I don't know what to say." Steen reached for Hanya's hand. "Your great aunt and I . . ."

"I don't think you have to tell me."

He nodded.

"Good for you," I lied.

What can Hanya see in a cop?

"Thank you for understanding," Hanya grinned weakly.

Maybe he's good in bed?

The thought made me smile, but I contained my laughter. I recalled a few random psychological theories of sexual attraction. Some researchers believed that we're attracted to faces that remind us of our parents or relatives. Others say that certain physical characteristics arouse pre-programmed preferences. Nature or nurture? Most agreed that sexual attraction is intensified during states of strong emotion or high anxiety.

Robert and me. Steen and Hanya. Maybe it was predictable?

New Agers and spiritualists believed in soul mates – people who had been parted in past lives – and found each other again as in reincarnation and *gilgul*. Some called it "working out Karma." Others claimed that past lives determined sexuality. There was even an entire literary genre devoted to sexual tensions between people whose past lives intersected. They called it *Paranormal Romance*.

Hanya hated the stuff.

"Would you like to have dinner with . . . us?" Hanya asked but didn't mean it.

"No. I have work to do," I said too quickly.

There was a long, tense silence.

No one knew what to say next.

4

My cell broke the silence. It was a text from Robert.

Want 2 fuck?

I giggled.

Not now. Will explain ltr

I glanced at Hanya and Steen. They stared at each other, both obviously unhappy about my intrusion.

u r missing a good thing

No Robert. I'm not missing anything.

Call u ltr

"I think," I said slowly to Hanya and Steen, "that we need to talk. After that, I'll leave you alone so you can get back to . . ." I giggled like a little kid.

Hanya sighed. Steen looked annoyed.

Maybe I will see Robert later.

5

Hanya and Steen waited.

I glanced at a skyscraper hovering above us, as if judging our truths and lies.

"Did you tell him?" I asked Hanya.

"No."

"Tell me what?"

"We agreed not to say anything."

"Tell me what, Hanya?"

Steen was irritated.

Hanya took a deep breath. "I followed Ayla."

"You what?"

She put her finger on his lips. "Sssssssh. I followed Ayla."

"Why?"

"Because I could."

Hanya told him the story about her trip to the Bronx, East Tremont, and Mack. "They kissed," she finished softly, "like us."

Steen was stunned. "*Nothing* like us. How could you keep that from me?"

"I was waiting for the right time."

"The right time? Are you crazy?"

Steen shook his head angrily as Hanya implored me with her eyes.

"She was going to tell you . . . It was my decision to keep it secret. I'm sorry." I wondered why I covered for Hanya. Perhaps I *liked* the two of them together?

"Do you think," Hanya whispered stupidly, "that it means anything?"

"Do you really expect me to answer that?" Steen growled. "I just don't know why you didn't tell me sooner."

"It proves that Ayla is the accomplice," I interjected.

"It proves nothing except that Ayla is still with Mack and meeting him secretly. Damn, Hanya, he could have killed you if he saw you watching."

"Remember what she said on the show," Hanya said quickly. "'I made a big mistake and now I want to make it better'? What was her real mistake? Loving a psychopath?"

"Many women have fallen in love with and married psychopathic killers – even after they're convicted." I added, thinking of Joshua.

It was much safer to be clinical.

"To some," Hanya added slowly, deliberately, "they're drawn to these men. It can be sexual, it can be a rescue fantasy, it can be the need to be part of the media spotlight . . ."

"Low self-esteem," I added professorially. "They align themselves against the world and defend their loved one. It's the beauty and the beast syndrome where they get close to danger without being hurt."

"Getting involved with violent men makes them feel stronger. Some want to collaborate with evil," Hanya's voice strengthened. "Remember Sondra London? She was involved with Gerard Schaefer, who confessed to abducting, torturing, and killing nearly 110 people; Keith Jesperson, "the Happy Face Killer" who murdered at least eight women, and Danny Rolling, the "Gainesville Ripper" who murdered and raped at least eight people, including five students – known for mutilating victim's bodies and posing them to intensify the carnage."

"Richard Ramirez – the Night Stalker – found guilty of 13 counts of murder, 5 counts of attempted murder, and 11 sexual assaults – married Doreen Lioy when he was on Death Row – in the visiting room at San Quentin. The bride wore a calf-length white wedding dress with lace sleeves. The groom wore starched prison blues."

"Judith Mawson described her husband, Gary Ridgway – the Green River Serial Killer believed to have murdered 70 people – as the 'perfect husband.'"

"What about Charles Manson and *his* women?"

Steen listened, amazed. "Enough! You're both nuts."

We paused.

"What?" Hanya asked flatly.

"Drown yourself in psychobabble. Avoid the fact that Ayla and Mack are up to something."

I frowned. "Maybe Ayla and Mack are still together . . ."

"Ayla is the accomplice?" Hanya hissed.

"Maybe," he sighed. "Maybe not. We don't have any real proof."

"Who else?"

He shrugged. "You know the list."

I stared at the skyscraper. Was there a message in its other-worldliness? A word rose in my head; an internal painting in my mind. *Why?*

6

I left Hanya and Steen alone on the terrace. They looked relieved.

I went through the living room, grabbed a *Chocolate Works* rum truffle and texted Robert. It was an interesting pairing.

Want company?
K
In 20?
Ready.

The flavor of the chocolate and rum lingered in my mouth as I cabbed uptown to Robert's apartment.

Robert buzzed me into his apartment. He said nothing, pulled me inside and bit my neck. "What would you like this time?" He laughed, pressing me against the closed door.

"Wait." I pushed him away. "I want to talk."

"Talk," he leered. "Dirty talk? You're a hooker and I'm a high-paying John today. I'm going to make you . . ."

"Stop. I mean really talk, not play."

Robert growled.

I slipped away, moving to the black couch, not far from the *Kama Sutra* porcelain sculptures. Robert took it as an invite.

"Whore," Robert screamed, and lunged at me. "I'm paying you to fuck, not talk."

He pushed me down on the couch and pulled up my *Alexander Wang* stripe knit top, burying his head in my breasts.

I laughed and squirmed away. "Give me a few minutes."

"I'm paying you for . . ."

"Stop. We'll do what you want." I rolled away, stood up, and yanked down my shirt. Robert scowled, grabbed, and I stepped out of his reach.

"Soon."

"Okay, I get it. The torture of delayed gratification."

"Whatever you want to call it." His eyes glistened and he reached out for me. I backed further away, toward the kitchen. Robert paused, rubbing his hands together like a predator readying for the kill.

I lay my hands on the cool black granite counter and took a deep breath.

"I want to ask you about the case."

"What?"

"The case – your documentary – the whole deal."

He took a deep breath and leaned back into the couch. Resigned. "What do you want to know?"

"Do you know Mack's accomplice?"

"Why would I know?"

"Maybe a guess?"

"I tape, not investigate. That's Steen's job."

I thought of Hanya and Steen and struggled not to smile. "You've been in on this from the beginning. You must have some theories."

"I don't like mysteries."

"This isn't a mystery. It's real life."

He shook his head. "I don't trust Visch."

"Visch?"

"Yeah. I don't trust him."

"Why would Visch care?"

"He's into Griet."

"Are they a couple?"

Robert laughed. "No, Visch is gay. He's into Griet for other reasons."

"What?"

"Visch wants his own show so he sticks by Griet. He'll do anything for her. The guy is a total foodie."

I shook my head and glanced down at the black granite. There was a black-framed photo of The Senator standing between Robert and a woman. She had the same caramel-colored hair as Robert, but otherwise looked different. Softer. There was something about her face, the way she peered into the camera that was oddly familiar.

"Who is she?" I held up the photo.

Robert grinned. "Are you jealous, bitch?"

"I'm just asking."

"No fun," he grumbled. "That's Kiran, my twin sister. My *fraternal* twin. You can't get two people more different than us."

"She looks so familiar."

"She should."

"Why?"

"She was the shrink that worked with your cousin Joshua."

I dropped the photo. It shattered on the granite countertop. I stared at the pieces, trying to make sense of what Robert had just revealed.

Robert was done. He leaped from the couch and grabbed me. "If you're going to be my hooker, bitch, I want to get started *now*."

I couldn't get Robert's words from my head.

She was the shrink that worked with your cousin Joshua.

Did Robert know that all along? Did Griet? Why would anyone want to mix the two – bring Robert to my doorstep? It was as if they were resurrecting my family's infamous past when Grandma Espie faced the wolves. Why didn't anyone tell me?

I touched the hamsa on my neck. It was hot.

As Robert took me, I saw Hanya and Steen kissing beneath the gaze of Mack, blood dripping from his eyes. Watching? Waiting?

"I'm going to fuck you kike," Robert roared, "like you've never been fucked before."

I immersed myself in the present; a lone shadow stretched across a broken road.

7

The next day Griet called a meeting.

We gathered at Munsee Court for safety concerns. Griet arrived with Visch and the warm-up crew, Jen, Mia, and Shane. I wondered why she brought them but said nothing. Tamirah watched, an annoying smirk on her face. Hanya, Ayla, and I sat on the couch. Robert stood to the side, directing Isobel to shoot the scene. Steen hung back, studying the group. What was in his head? Did he suspect another conspiracy? Was he staring too hard at Ayla? Hanya slyly glanced at him. He ran his tongue over his lips.

Robert was aloof, professional, and doing his job.

I brought a small wooden box of frozen, square cocoa covered truffles – *Chocolate Works* specialty – and offered it to everyone. No one touched it but me. I took a bite and buttery chocolate filled my mouth – a lovely distraction from the business at hand.

"I invited you here," Griet began, her gaunt face tightened into a scowl, "to discuss the dangers of starting up *Truth With Dr. H!*"

"Is there a return date?" Hanya cried.

"Not yet. However, we're being inundated with email, voice mail, and internet rumors *complaining* that viewers are being unjustly punished for one man's actions."

I glanced at Ayla. Her face was unreadable.

"There's pressure to return to the air," Griet continued. "Our good Steen has informed me that there is danger. We need to consider the best way to proceed."

All eyes turned to Steen. He glanced at Hanya then looked away. *What was* he *hiding?*

"There's danger for each of us," Griet gritted her teeth. Her thin lips contorted into a grimace. "Even you." She glanced at the warm-up crew, Jen, Mia, and Shane. We all knew she didn't care about the young people. This was Griet's show and she skillfully choreographed everyone to achieve her end.

"We're good," Shane spoke for all of them.

Griet nodded as if it was a question of life-and-death.

"This situation can turn into a one-time event or it can distort everything that comes after. We have to be cautious. Mr. Visch?"

The attorney stepped forward. I thought of Robert's words.

I don't trust Visch. He's into Griet. Visch wants his own show so he sticks by her and will do anything . . .

"Litigation," Visch said as if he were announcing the presence of royalty. "We need to avoid litigation."

No one responded.

"If we start too soon – choose the wrong subject or guests – we can be faced with a lawsuit."

"And jeopardize our main sponsor, FRS," Griet added.

Robert frowned.

"What do you mean?" Hanya asked.

"Gentle," Visch chided. "We need to be conciliatory. Not give the wrong people an opportunity."

"Opportunity for what?" Hanya retorted.

"You have to be calm, dear," Griet patronized.

"I don't want to be calm. I want my show back."

As if to challenge Hanya, Griet turned to Ayla. "How do you *feel* about that?"

Ayla reddened.

Maybe you should ask Mack.

"I . . . don't . . . know . . . ," she stuttered.

"Perhaps you should be consulted after Hanya meets with her production team." Griet snarled.

"What?" Hanya blurted. "That's a violation of my rights . . ."

"We're not discussing rights here," Visch said stiffly. "We're talking about safety."

Money.

Everyone began talking at once. Arguing. Should the show return to the air? Should it have the same subject matter? Should it be "cleansed" to avoid litigation? The babble of voices was deafening. I glanced at Robert. He grinned and licked his lips. I looked at Steen. He couldn't take his eyes off of Hanya.

Then I saw it.

Visch and Griet stared at each other. They shook their heads in approval.

This was exactly what they wanted. Anticipation was sure to increase ratings. Keep the audience, the bloggers, newscasters, and social media going strong.

8

The next day was predictable. No one saw it except in hindsight.

I had too many questions and no answers. The hamsa felt warm against my skin as if trying to tell me something. What? What was I missing in the melee? Hanya remained in her bedroom, refusing to speak to anyone. The meeting had ended without a decision – exactly what Griet and Visch wanted. *Truth With Dr. H!* had no start date and no plan. Griet roused everyone, including the media.

It was as if someone was manipulating the entire operation.

Reports of the meeting were everywhere – broadcast TV, newspapers on and offline, and radio. Social media was buzzing with debates. Should *Truth With Dr. H!* return before Mack was apprehended? Was Griet Vansalee drumming up anticipation and ratings? The show had become a new genre – a mix of crime drama, reality, and tabloid T.V.

The worst was You Tube. A video of Dr H crying, "that's a violation of my rights . . ." went viral. Even Anderson Cooper added it to his *RidicuList*.

I tried to rethink my relationship with Robert. Why did he release the video? Was he working with Griet? The Senator? I had no idea where I fit into his life, other than the breathless sex games. He always responded when I needed him but what good did he really do? I wondered whether Robert was an opportunist like the others.

How did he *know* that his sister had been Joshua's therapist? Didn't that violate patient confidentiality? Had he actually researched my family?

The situation was out of control, without anyone interested in stemming the tide of theories, invectives, or rumors as if they savored being on the digital lips of scandal mongers and conspiracy theorists. There was something incongruent – I was missing a piece. What? Was I paranoid? I rethought the screenplay. There was only one person who didn't offer her opinion.

Moeda.

She remained in a coma. It made no sense to visit her again but I didn't know what else to do. I knocked on Hanya's bedroom door and told her I was headed for the library. There was only a muffled response. I made my way out of the condo, glancing at the now-empty terrace. For a moment I saw Hanya and Steen kissing. I smiled. It was strange and awkward but honest. At least that was what I believed when I left Munsee Court that morning. I barely acknowledged Remez, and headed to the subway. The doorman hadn't said anything to me since the day I discovered Hanya and Steen. Doormen were like bartenders and hairdressers – they kept secrets.

I hoped that visiting the hospital – being in the presence of the true victim – would give me some clues. I needed to figure out what was happening and what to do next. An unconscious Moeda might magically lead me to a new set of theories. I crossed Bowling Green and took the subway uptown, oblivious to the noise and people around me.

The hospital was busy with normal mid-morning activities. Nurses, aides, doctors, maintenance people, technicians, volunteers, and an occasional teary-eyed visitor bustled through the corridors. No one noticed me. I paused at the desk, waiting for the nurse behind the computer screen to acknowledge me.

"How is Moeda?"

"The same," the nurse said, her eyes briefly leaving the computer screen. She shifted her chubby body on the too-small chair. "You have to be patient." Her voice was a monotone. "People in this condition, GSW – gunshot wound to the head – are difficult to predict. They can be normal or . . ." she didn't need the words.

Or die. Or remain comatose. Or be physically and mentally disabled.

"Or recover," the nurse met my eyes. "No one really knows."

I shrugged. "Thank you."

She returned to her computer.

No one really knew. That was the best the medical world had to offer. As much as we knew about neurological function, there was so much more missing. There *were* miracles in our limited experience – situations we would describe as complete recoveries. There was also everything in between. As a psychologist, I knew too much about neurological damage to hold significant hope that Moeda would fully recover. The brain is an exquisitely designed structure, able to heal or compensate for many different traumas. She had been in a coma for 20 days, suggesting a poor prognosis.

I took a deep breath and headed for Moeda's room.

Suddenly I felt a burning sensation on my chest. It was the hamsa. I paused, touching the charm. It was vibrating.

What are you trying to tell me?

I knew it was all silly paranormal superstition – New Age stuff. I was a scientist and didn't believe in anything that couldn't be documented, tested, and analyzed by research. I lived by operational definitions, statistical analyses, and painstakingly established probabilities to navigate my world of diagnosis, assessment, and intervention. Believing that a hamsa could tell me anything was pure fantasy – a pleasant illusion that had no bearing on reality.

Yet the hamsa was hot. There was no denying *that*.

"Grandma Espie," I whispered to no one. "Are you here?"

I laughed at myself as I recalled her voice from the not-too-distant past.

"I have something for you, Sage."

Grandma put the hamsa on my neck.

"It's protected me all my life . . . repelled the evil eye and the angel of death. The hamsa served me well. Mother gave it to me – and her mother gave it to her before that. Hundreds of years reaching back to Esperanza, our ancestor who was expelled from Spain."

I smiled, tears filling my eyes.

"You're the one with red hair and hazel eyes. The same as my red hair and hazel eyes and all the Esperanza's before us. Their spirits . . . Mother's spirit . . . and my spirit . . . are here. We'll protect you from wherever we are. When it's your time, give it to someone you love very much. Someone who needs its protection."

"I can't . . ."

"You have no choice, Sage. It's my time to give it to you . . . and your time to take it."

A few days later, my grandmother was dead.

I shook off the image of Grandma Espie and her gift. It was a lovely thought but pure fiction. In my world, the only power held by the hamsa was sentimental. *But . . .*

Did I really need protection? Wasn't Hanya the target? Or Ayla?

I took a deep breath and continued down the corridor to Moeda's room.

9

I was a shadow. No one saw me or cared.

I peeked into rooms, catching glimpses of the sick and injured, people in pain. Many were old and fragile, their skin stretched so thin they looked like living corpses. Others were younger, with pale faces and resigned eyes, staring at carefully placed TV screens. The hospital smells made me shudder – antiseptic and decay, illness and depression. It reminded me of an old *Star Trek* episode where the doctor described modern medicine as "barbaric." Yes, this was barbaric – along with the scene that had brought me here to visit Moeda.

My hamsa burned hotter.

Shaking my head, I approached Moeda's room.

Someone touched my arm.

"So sorry," an elderly volunteer in a pink uniform said. "What a waste of a young life."

I looked into her watery eyes.

"It's a shame," she continued, "it's so rare that someone comes out of a deep coma like that. A real shame."

"Thank you," I mumbled and moved on.

I approached Moeda's room expecting silence pierced by the electronic buzz of machines.

I froze.

There were voices.

10

Two voices spoke softly to one another. I peered in the door so they couldn't see me.

It was Ayla talking to Moeda.

And Moeda responding.

I shook my head, not believing what I saw or heard.

"It's working really well," Ayla said softly.

"As we planned," Moeda agreed. "I just don't know how long I can do this. Some of *them* are beginning to suspect."

"As long as necessary," Ayla said sharply. "He shot you, not the other way around. This has made us famous around the world. The baby can't avoid the news. He'll come forward."

My heart pounded wildly. I rushed back to the nurse's station. "She's awake," I cried to the chubby, brown-eyed nurse. "She's talking."

"I was just there," the nurse remained fixed on her computer.

"Come look. I just heard her talking to her daughter."

Reluctantly, the nurse rose. "Let me see."

I raced back into Moeda's room. Ayla was there, standing over her mother. Moeda was – comatose.

"I just heard . . ." I began.

A few tears trickled down Ayla's face. "No change," she said.

The nurse went over to the bed and fluffed the pillows. "Do you hear me?" she asked Moeda. "Your daughter and a friend are here to visit. Would you like to say hello?"

No response.

"I just heard them talking to each other."

Ayla glared at me.

"Sometimes," the nurse said evenly, "we hear what we want . . . not the truth."

"That *is* the truth."

"I'm sorry, ma'am. There's been no change since I last checked her. You can see that for yourself."

"But I heard them . . ."

The nurse patted my shoulder. "I'll be at the desk if you need me." She left the room, sighing.

Ayla and I glared at one another.

"I heard you and Moeda," I said softly.

"You were imagining things." Ayla responded, a smirk in her eyes.

"I heard . . ."

"Look."

I looked at Moeda. I waited. She didn't stir.

"I know what I heard."

"Sometimes we hear what we want and not the truth," Ayla mimicked the nurse.

"You're hiding something."

"What can I possibly hide?" Silver screen tears coursed down her face. "My mother is dying. That's all I care about."

"I don't believe you. I know what I heard."

Ayla sobbed so loud the nurse returned to the room. "Why are you upsetting her?" She demanded.

"I just heard them . . ."

"Enough." The nurse said firmly. "If you insist on upsetting them, I'll have to ask you to leave."

I glanced at Ayla. She sneered.

"Of course. I don't want to upset anyone."

The nurse left and I lingered silently for 20 long minutes. I counted every breath, noted every movement. Nothing. Ayla remained by Moeda's bedside, shifting her eyes between her mother and me.

"I'm going home," I said finally.

"Good idea."

I left Moeda and Ayla, pausing in the corridor. I decided to wait. Suddenly I heard Ayla whispering. The words were hard to understand.

"We have to be more careful."

I was stunned.

There was no response.

I had an idea. I rushed down the corridor and out of the hospital. I headed to the public library to use their computers. I didn't want anyone to know what I was researching.

11

Some called it false coma, others labeled it psychogenic coma. The screen documented everything I suspected. One neurologist, Dr. Roth, wrote:

Someone can fake a coma. It's not particularly uncommon. You can see it in people with Conversion Hysteria and also Malingerers. Some people are really good at it and fool doctors, family, and friends.

There are tricks and tests that can be used to help separate the "real" from the false – but how well they work depends on the knowledge and sophistication of the patient.

I stared at the words.

My head hurt from the questions.

Was Moeda faking a coma with Ayla's help? Where did Mack fit in, along with his mysterious accomplice?

Was Griet part of the scheme? Where did Visch and Tamirah fit in the scenario? Robert? Even The Senator seemed suspect.

Did Hanya *know*?

Nothing added up. Was I delusional or was there a conspiracy?

I didn't know where to turn or who to trust. If Moeda was faking a coma, were they searching for something *more* than a baby abandoned over 20 years ago? Maybe they were looking for money or their 15 minutes of fame?

I googled "why people go on reality shows" and discovered page after page of opinions from psychologists and participants; viewers and amateur sleuths. Most fed into the cultural concept that being on the screen glorified life – a "guest" received recognition and celebrity, both positive and negative. Unknown *regular* people have the opportunity to show themselves to the world, with the accompanying fantasy of fame, money, power, and grandiosity. The tradeoff was a public show of obscenity, crude entertainment, and exploitation.

Producers were pressured to maintain ratings in a fiercely competitive market. Strong-armed editing was one of their main tools. It didn't matter how their guests appeared – the unscripted format had to air as drama. The parameters were clear – shocking content raised ratings. Controversy, breaching privacy, sensationalism, macabre behavior, surreal true-life stories, and scandal – the list of lurid features edited for salacious audience consumption was endless. Jerry Springer once said that his show "unearths the most mind-blowing headlines in the supermarket tabloids, exposing the biggest stories of the day."

Truth With Dr. H! was a natural.

Along with *Dr. Phil* and the army of media shrinks who profess knowledge, information, and *education* for viewing audiences, the show fed into a public obsession with "magical" data. It provided "answers" from a wise, gentle sage with a lot of fancy titles. The doc *had* to know.

No one seemed concerned with how much media shrinks actually knew, experienced, or researched. If they had titles, made diagnoses, and offered erudite counsel on TV, it *had* to be true – all free of charge.

Griet Vansalee lived that paradigm. She kept things hot to compete with other media psychologists. Broadcast therapy was the drug of pop interventions. Reality was thriving – viewers disregarded the fact that it was staged, taped, and edited to feed their appetites between commercials. As viewers sat in their homes, plagued by their own issues, they dined on answers that lured them into a universal comfort zone.

How bad can I be *when those guests are so crazy?*

The *true* question was whether Griet and Visch created the entire scenario. Were Ayla and Moeda paid to cooperate? Who else was involved? Steen, Tamirah, Robert, Isobel?

Social media buzzed with speculations on when the show would return. The NYPD statements about the perpetrator "not yet apprehended" fed into the tension. It was great fun, along with the peripheral stuff like Steen finding Hanya; Robert finding me and becoming my sex buddy; and endless speculations on how FRS and The Senator would respond.

Was it all scripted or were we all victims of our own greed?

Did Mack have one accomplice or all of us?

The mystery took on a life of its own; internet bookies eagerly took bets.

12

I had an eerie dream that night. The sun burst through dark clouds and trees as Ayla and Moeda conspired an evil plot. Hanya and Steen ran away. Griet and Visch danced, in a pile of dollars, beneath the sun; Mallah and Remez, with fistfuls of cash, raced down between the trees, laughing wildly. Robert wandered along the East River, surrounded by crowds, flashing his camera and smile. The Senator watched from a safe distance.

I awoke, sweaty and frustrated. What about me?

It felt like everyone had perks but me.

It was time to shift the scale in my favor and devise a new strategy. I came up with a flawless plan that morning, lying in my bed and staring at the rooftops through the window. Life was going to get a lot better.

First, I would change my doctoral dissertation to violence in postmodern tabloid TV, using Robert's documentary, the social media posts, and You Tube as primary resources. My internship provided direct observational data to validate the research literature. The university mentors would love the concept, knowing *they* would also look good commercially *and* in academia. Perhaps one might publish a paper on mentoring doctoral students in postmodern research in tabloid media – lots of words and limited meaning.

Maybe *I* would write that article. I could start my own blog to further promote *me*.

The on and offline media would eagerly pick up and spread the results of my research. I would be interviewed on TV, the Internet, radio, press, and blogs. They would identify me as the newest and youngest expert in media psychology. Using the publicity, I would dummy-down my dissertation and publish my first commercial book in print and ebook. It would be destined to become an *Amazon* bestseller. I even had a catchy title:

Broken.

I grinned. Suddenly my future had new potential. The path was clear – I could never *be* a media psychologist but I could be their whistleblower. I touched my hair, wondering how the red would look under studio lights and in You Tube videos. Maybe I would work on a diet – scrape off the ten pounds that cameras add. A few regular days in the gym or a Zumba class might speed the process.

I took a deep breath. "I'm a professional," I said out loud to no one.

The room around me was silent; my hamsa was cold. What did *that* mean? I shook my head and outlined my approach. The first step was to meet everyone in Moeda's hospital room and blow her cover. I checked off the guest list: Hanya, Ayla, Moeda, Robert, Isobel, Steen, Tamirah, Griet, and Visch. All cozy in a safe hospital room with the camera rolling and a fake coma patient. The exploiters *exploited*.

I felt like a hero. I thought of other famous whistleblowers like Daniel Ellsberg who leaked the Pentagon Papers in 1971, exposing the classified secrets behind the Vietnam War. Mark Felt, a.k.a "Deep Throat" who exposed the infamous Watergate scandal, toppling Richard Nixon's presidency in 1974. Jeffrey Wigand, a former tobacco company executive, who divulged how cigarette companies intentionally packed their products with addictive levels of nicotine. Sherron Watkins, who revealed Enron Corporation's financial lies and frauds and was later named *Time* magazine's "Person of the Year." Bradley Manning, an Army intelligence analyst, who released classified military documents to *WikiLeaks* to "document the true costs of the wars in Iraq and Afghanistan," and Edward Snowden, a technical NSA and CIA contractor, who made public the details of classified U.S. mass surveillance programs.

Heroes or traitors? Either way, I liked their infamous club.

13

It was a strange day. The air was thick making it hard to breathe. It had been 22 days since Mack shot Moeda. Enough time for everyone to glean their rewards.

Outside, there was a city inversion, bringing a gray stillness and other-worldly feeling to the air. It was like moving through a sci-fi flick. In an inversion, air movement stalls and warm air and pollutants are trapped at the ground, making it difficult to breathe. Air quality alarms were triggered – *limit outdoor activity.* Feature stories of famous inversions were rehashed, like Salt Lake City's "mother of all inversions," and New York's 1966 Thanksgiving inversion where the weather was responsible for almost 200 deaths.

For a short time, the weather took precedence over local murders, rapes, riots in the Middle East, airplane crashes, and massacres by aging dictators. People on the street were hot and cranky; domestic violence increased; verbal and physical fights surged. The streets smelled and the mayor begged for patience. A heavy haze hung over the city.

"This will end," The Mayor said in a news conference. "Be patient and take caution."

When the inversion breaks, a violent thunderstorm erupts.

It was the perfect forecast.

Broken
By
Truth

1

We met in Moeda's hospital room. It was the end of the day and what I believed, the end of the story.

I was wrong.

Moeda lay still, eyes closed, faking her coma.

Ayla arrived in *Eileen Fischer* slim black ankle pants and *Jimmy Choo* comic patent pumps, paid for by the studio. Hanya selected a *Haute Hippie* silk blazer over *Phillip Lim* black pencil trousers. I wore my favorite jeans – the ones that Robert had stripped off multiple times.

We circled Moeda's bed like killer whales trapping a desperate sea lion on an ice floe.

A few minutes later, Griet and Visch appeared. Griet wore a funky beige *Donna Karan* open weave beach sweater with long sleeves and no shoulders. Her nails were painted turquoise. Visch looked his usual, in suit and yellow tie with a chili sauce stain. Tamirah followed, clutching her briefcase.

No one spoke.

We watched Moeda. I wondered how the woman could bear so many eyes on her without flinching. Finally, Robert and Isobel joined us. Robert patted my shoulder and Isobel, dressed in a cheap pink tee and jeans, set up the camera by the open door.

"Where's Steen?" I asked Hanya.

"How would I know?"

Everyone was eerily silent. The red light appeared on the camera. Isobel was taping.

"Should we wait for him?" Visch asked impatiently.

"We should," I said, but no one agreed.

"We don't need the NYPD in on this discussion," Ayla snarled. "What good would he do?"

"Are you kidding?" Hanya's voice was high pitched. "We still have to find Mack. Until we find him, there's no show . . ."

"I never said that."

All eyes turned to Griet.

"I said . . ." Griet paused, "that we should *cautiously* consider how to proceed."

"We want everyone to be safe," Visch added quietly.

"Of course," Hanya retorted. "That's why we *need* him here."

Who needs whom, Auntie?

"What do you think, Sage?"

Everyone looked at me. Were we better with or without The Detective? "I don't think it makes much difference. He'll be here soon – he won't really miss anything."

Hanya glared at me.

2

"Why did you ask us all to meet *here*?" Griet demanded.

"I want to show you something."

"What?"

"Moeda," I said loudly, "is faking."

There was dead silence.

"Faking what?" Ayla whispered.

"She's not in a coma. I heard you and Moeda talking."

"The doctors . . ."

"You can fake a coma so well that many doctors can't tell or, at best, aren't sure."

"My mother wouldn't fake . . ."

I shrugged. "Isn't it time to come clean, Ayla? Tell us why you and your mother really got involved in this?"

"What are you talking about?"

"Is it the money, Ayla? Fame? Some kind of crazy scheme to alleviate guilt? Or are both of you Mack's accomplices?"

"How dare you."

I wove the story. "You, Mack, and Moeda planned the whole thing. Imagine the power and money that would be yours. The problem is that Mack is a lousy shot and hit the target when he wasn't supposed to."

Tamirah chuckled. "It would make a good *Lifetime* movie."

I glared at her. "There probably wasn't even a baby born – just a lie."

A new voice, deep, masculine and thinned with age, came from the door. "I wouldn't waste my time with the bitch."

We all turned.

3

Mack stood at the entrance to the hospital room.

I recognized him immediately from the show and You Tube. There was no mistaking the white hair, blank eyes, and the tip of his chest-wide Nazi Iron Eagle tattoo peeking above his tee shirt.

Everyone froze.

"I came here to tell you," Mack said softly, staring at Ayla, "that I love you. If you want, *I'll* help you find the kid. You and me."

Ayla's face melted.

"Come with me. Leave the bitch. I have the bike outside and we'll get out of this place. Away from these people who want to hurt you so they can make the big bucks."

He stepped across the room and reached for Ayla, pushing me aside. Beneath his tee shirt was a bulge – a gun tucked into his shirt. Ayla stared, mesmerized, as he shoved first me, then Hanya, out of his path.

Isobel continued to tape.

Mack was strong and I stumbled. Robert stepped forward to steady me, wrapping his arm across my breasts.

"Public fucking," he whispered in my ear.

Mack reached Ayla and grabbed her arm. "Come with me," he roared.

Suddenly, like a dead woman rising from a coffin, Moeda sat up and screamed.

4

"No. Not again." Moeda wailed.

Mack pulled Ayla into his arms. She didn't resist.

"Noooooooooo," Moeda howled.

Robert nuzzled my neck.

"You promise?" Ayla asked Mack. "To help me find him?"

"Yes," Mack responded. "If you come with me."

Moeda grabbed Ayla's arm with surprising strength. "We'll find him *my* way," she cried. "All these people – they'll help. You'll have your son back . . . power, money, fame . . ."

"Without Mack?" Ayla peeled Moeda's fingers off her arm. "We belong together."

Mack laughed. "Bitch," he spat at Moeda and dragged Ayla to the door.

Steen arrived.

Oddly, Steen didn't try to stop Mack and Ayla. He was looking past the door and Moeda.

What's he doing?

Robert held me tighter, kissing my neck. "This couldn't be planned," he said maniacally.

I tried to push him away but he was too strong.

And it was crazy, wild . . . fun.

"On the hospital bed," Robert laughed in my ear.

I looked over his shoulder as the camera clattered to the floor. Steen lunged, but he was too late.

Isobel pointed a tiny pink limited edition *Kahr P380* pistol with stainless steel slide. It was a beautiful, delicately designed weapon for the discerning woman. Pretty and pink. I visualized the advertising copy.

Feminine but deadly.

Made for the woman who needs to protect herself from invading men.

Invading men? Who were the invaders in this broken scene?

My hamsa felt like a hot iron on my neck. Was my life flashing before me as I faced death?

A strange genealogy careened through my mind, rather than a flashback. It was a timeweb of the women who wore the hamsa as they struggled through life. A predatory human hovered, tensed to kill. Red-headed Esperanza, in 15th century garb, led a child into a steaming jungle. A brown-skinned slave girl with crimson hair and hazel eyes stared at the East River. A teenage Grandma Espie played on a teeming Bronx Street.

And me. Begging Joshua to eat chocolate.

5

Isobel didn't hesitate. A crazed smile twisted her lips, as she aimed the gun at Robert. "I loved you," she cried. "I loved you and if I can't have you, no one will."

The shot reverberated through the room. Steen leaped at Isobel and seemed to hover in mid-air. He knocked the gun out of Isobel's hand, but it was too late. "I loved you, Robert," Isobel cried, falling across Moeda on the bed, powerless beneath Steen's weight.

Hanya, Griet, Visch, Tamirah, and Moeda didn't move as if caught in a freeze frame. Mack and Ayla fled through the door and down the hallway. I could hear the clatter of carts as they pushed everything and everyone out of their way.

In my head, I heard a click on the pause button – a stop on the You Tube Video. Enough time to realize that Mack never had an actual accomplice. Perhaps in some strange way, he was also a victim. We were all supporting characters. There was another – a shadowy figure that used our own demons to control us. God? Satan? The Prince of Darkness?

6

At first, I didn't realize that Robert was no longer holding me.

I was holding him.

We dropped to the floor. My head was blank. The images fled as quickly as they appeared.

"Sage," Hanya screamed.

Outside, the inversion broke. Thunder and lightning shook the city. Rain pelted the windows. Mack would have a tricky time on his bike.

Everything went dark.

7

I awoke on a gurney in the emergency room. I didn't know how I got there. Hanya ticked off the facts, one-by-one, in a shaky voice.

Robert was dead.

Isobel was in handcuffs.

Ayla and Mack were gone.

Moeda stopped faking her coma.

Hanya held my hand as they treated me for a gunshot wound that would have killed me if it hadn't been for Robert's body. The bullet went straight through his heart, vampire-style. By the time it reached me, there was only superficial damage. A lot of blood, a few stitches, and a scar I would wear for the rest of my life.

Like Mack's Nazi Iron Eagle tattoo.

The hamsa was bent, as if it deflected the bullet. I knew a blue and silver charm which protected the wearer against the "evil eye" didn't have the power to fight off a bullet. I *knew* but I wasn't sure; science abandoned me.

The rest of the story was TV Theater. Once Isobel was subdued, Griet and Visch dove for the camera. Ignoring Steen's orders, they taped the scene then fled. Later in the day, they posted the You Tube Video.

It lasted 3.4 minutes and went viral.

8

Robert's funeral was a media event. It was staged six days after the shooting – enough time to be discreet but not too long to lose public interest.

There were politicians from New York City, Albany, and Washington. The Vice President of The United States appeared, appropriately sad-faced, offering her condolences and pausing in front of the camera to hug The Senator. Bill Clinton showed up with his entourage, grasping The Senator's hand as he patted his back and whispered something the mikes couldn't pick up. Other celebrities attended, faces painted in sympathy as they play-acted yet another role. A contingent of Broadway actors made an appearance, smiling woefully for the cameras.

The media was present en masse, with cameras, questions, mikes, computers, and endless sound bytes. The news would feature stories surrounding the event for another week until, like all scoops, it withered beneath newer and hotter headlines. Within a year, tell-all books would hit the bestseller lists, ghost-written titles by Griet, Hanya, and Visch. Their content would be featured repeatedly in the media.

The Senator, with his caramel-colored hair and blue eyes played his role expertly.

"I'm devastated," he said tearfully to the media. "My family and I will all dearly miss Robert, my talented and highly respected son. New York and the FRS family will mourn his passing – a life taken suddenly, brutally, and unnecessarily."

His voice was measured, his words sprinkled with carefully placed sobs. His face was delicately contorted with pain although his eyes were blank and flat like Robert's.

He was what Robert would have looked like in thirty years.

I shivered.

"I think," The Senator added, tinged with choreographed anger, "it's time to consider stronger gun laws. We need to protect the families of America. I'm going to propose a new measure . . ."

It sounded like his next campaign tag line.

Kiran, Robert's fraternal twin, stood tearfully by her mother. Behind her were her husband, rumored to be a fireman, two sons, and daughter. They all had the family's caramel-colored hair and blue eyes. Only the eldest son had the flat, emotionless eyes of his uncle and grandfather.

They seemed saddened by Robert's death but in an odd way, not surprised.

"Robert was just like his father," Kiran said in a brief comment to the press. "We'll all miss him."

Just like his father.

Every broadcast and cable news channel featured her comment. Millions of posts materialized in blogs, Twitter, Reddit, and Face Book. The Senator's top aide set up a memorial web page – TheSenatorsSonIsdead.com – complete with old photos (mostly of father and son), comments, clips from Robert's work, and a page to leave messages. Ultimately, two million people from around the world left their condolences, making it one of the most active websites for the week. Celebrity tweeters joined the melee, including Anderson Cooper, Oprah Winfrey, Ellen DeGeneres, Kanye West, and Lady Gaga. Everyone wanted to be part of the show.

I attended the funeral with Hanya, Steen, Tamirah, Griet, and Visch. Moeda remained in the hospital for psychiatric evaluation; Ayla and Mack were gone; and Isobel exchanged pink for beige at the juvenile detention center on Rikers Island. The island had been named for Abraham Rycken, a Dutchman who moved to Long Island in 1638. The land was now home to one of the most notorious jails in the country. I never knew that Isobel was barely eighteen years old. It was reported that she was under suicide watch.

The service for Robert was held at Trinity Church.

Trinity was built on land that was originally a Dutch burial ground. It had a stunning view straight down Wall Street. The first church was built in 1697 – two other structures followed. Presently, the church was the third largest landowner in New York – after the city and the Catholic Church. Many famous Americans were buried at Trinity's cemetery – most recently, beloved Jewish mayor, Ed Koch, who reportedly paid $20,000 for the plot in 2008, five years before his death. Mayor Koch had his gravestone engraved with the *Shema,* in English and Hebrew.

Hear O Israel, the Lord our God, the Lord is One.

Koch added the final words of Daniel Pearl, the Wall Street Journal reporter murdered in Pakistan, to his memorial:

My father is Jewish. My mother is Jewish. I am Jewish.

I decided that the same words would be carved into my tombstone.

Ironically, one of Trinity Cemetery's most famous residents, Alexander Hamilton, also died from a gunshot wound in a duel with Aaron Burr in 1894. Among his many memorials was the Alexander Hamilton U.S. Custom House at One Bowling Green.

I wondered if Robert would have any memorials.

It was a strange funeral. Every piece connected with another – a perfect end for The Senator's Son.

9

Hanya, Steen, Tamirah, and I walked to Trinity Church from Munsee Court. It was strange going to Robert's funeral so close to home.

Should I cry like the sister? Should I grimace like the father? How should I feel about a man who died in my arms and by doing so, saved my life?

I wondered about those seconds right before Isobel pulled the trigger. It wasn't a flashback of my life, but more like a timeweb of the women who wore the hamsa. What were their stories and how did they relate to me? Perhaps we *were* connected by something more than blood and an old blue and silver charm? *Gilgul*? I had no answers, only questions. Did the hamsa save me for a reason that stretched beyond the science I used to guide my life? Was there something that explained it all?

Clearly, I was broken.

By Truth, Birth, and Evil; Madness, Kings, and Men.

A voice, quiet and deep within, spoke loudly and firmly.

You have to find out.

I looked at Hanya. Find out what? The stories behind the images? The broken pieces? My genealogy? An old voice whispered in my head.

It's what we were destined to do – what God wants.

What was I supposed to do?

Review the facts. I never really *knew* Robert. At the same time, I knew him too well. I was numb, unable to figure out what to feel or think about anything that transpired since the shooting at *Truth With Dr. H!*

I thought of the dominoes in Robert's apartment and how I wasn't allowed to touch them. It made me think of the *dominoes effect* – a theory based on the chain reaction when a small change causes a similar change nearby, which causes another change . . . all in sequence. The dominoes theory was used during the Cold War, arguing that if one country in a region became communist, the other countries would follow. Many people applied this to Hitler and the fall of Europe; more recently, the Arab Spring of 2012. Mental health theorists used the dominoes effect to explain social behavior, saying that one human action will predictably lead to another given the right context.

Remove one piece and it can all be prevented. Keep the reaction going and events follow like a chain of dominoes, each one pushed down and in turn, pushing down its sequential neighbor.

Is that what this was about? *Dominoes?*

Was the human experience merely a dominoes sequence with traceable catalysts ranging from trauma and evil to strength and determination?

I turned this over and over in my head, trying to trace the path. If Robert's death was the result of the dominoes effect, who was the catalyst to initiate and set the ensuing events? Steen always thought it was Mack's accomplice, but Isobel acted on her own, independent of everyone but Robert. Were Ayla and Mack behind it? If so, how did Robert, Steen, and I get sucked into the plot?

I stared at the third and current Trinity Church, a classic Gothic Revival and National Historic Landmark. Its 280 foot bell tower and spire, once the tallest in the city, was now dwarfed by the skyscrapers. We entered through huge bronze doors into a hauntingly beautiful interior, featuring a magnificent nave with towering stained glass windows. The pews were crowded. As the service began, I couldn't get rid of the question.

Who put everything in motion? Who made sure it fell like dominoes?

There had to be someone else involved. I had to find out – even if it took research that stretched back 500 years.

"I'll help you," Hanya said softly, reading my thoughts. "We'll take this journey together."

I stared at her. Yes, Hanya and I would take this journey together. There was only one last place to go – one other person to check out. I was determined not to one stone remain unturned, however long it took. My family tree was haunted by psychopaths – both the murdering and non-murdering types. I had to know *who.*

It was my legacy.

Beyond
Truth

1

The Senator sat in his favorite luxury recliner chair – a custom-made power seat in dark mahogany leather. It was nestled in his spacious office on Park Avenue. Only he, the cleaning lady, and his staff were permitted into his sanctuary. His wife, children, grandchildren, and visitors were prohibited without appointments. Requests were filed with his secretary – a stern, homely woman who never smiled. She resided in a large waiting room, filled with his framed campaign posters, community service awards, FRS photographs, and political commendations. Plush seats, upscale magazines, and a muscled, uniformed security guard completed the scene.

The guard and secretary were gone for the day.

On the side table next to the recliner was a small box of old ivory dominoes.

He caressed the dominoes like a rosary, savoring the cool, smooth surface. The Senator closed his eyes and recalled what happened when she had first come to him with The *Perfect* Idea, nearly a year ago.

She had knocked on his office door. He expected her.

"Enter," he said sharply.

She opened the door and paused, framed by the outside light. She wasn't a good-looking woman; too old, bony, and severe for his tastes. He liked them young and hard.

"What brings you here?" He asked pleasantly.

Boldly, she left the door open. She approached his recliner. "You know. Power. Money. Ratings."

"Ratings?"

"They're dropping."

He nodded. "So?"

"I want it to stop. Reverse itself so I get more not less."

Their eyes locked.

"Why me?" He asked, amused.

"Dominoes," she clenched her jaw. "Our favorite game when we were kids in Levittown. You . . . me . . . and all we did to each other."

"Ah, yes. I remember those days. Such exquisite pleasure. It was when I first embraced the dominoes effect." He shook his head reverently. "Even as an adolescent, my vision went way beyond normal men. I knew that one human action will predictably lead to another, given the right context. Remove one piece and everything comes to a dead halt." The Senator preached to her, holding up a domino as if to demonstrate. "Keep the flow and events follow like a chain of dominoes, each one pushed down and in turn pushing down its neighbor. It has served me well."

"I know."

"How can my dominoes help *you*?"

She moved closer. "Remember those days, Dutchboy, hidden in your room? She leaned over and kissed his crotch. He pressed his hand lightly against the back of her head.

She backed off. "Would you like to play again?"

He shrugged.

She opened her mouth so he could see the red silicon spiked tongue stud that she had carefully selected for him. "For you." She stuck out her tongue.

Interesting, he thought.

"I need you and your dominoes. I'll do anything you want."

"I have what I want."

She ignored him. "I want you to make Dr. H! the biggest and most profitable show on TV. Ratings off the charts. Conspiracy theories going viral. Media exploding."

He ran the tip of his tongue over his lips. "How do you propose I do *that*?"

"I have The *Perfect* Idea. Straight from Dr. H herself. Only *you* can make it happen the way I want."

"Hanya? Does she know you're here?"

"Of course not. That's between us – like it's always been."

He rubbed his chin. "What do *I* get out of this?"

"On my knees."

It wasn't the first time, but the red silicon spiked tongue stud made it more intriguing.

She fell to her knees and unzipped his pants. He watched her placidly. He could have any woman he wanted but he liked her arrogance.

"Deal," he sighed.

The sport was foreseeing who would be the victim. That was the part he loved – violence that wasn't completely predictable, only probable, requiring titillating calculations. The variables delighted him; he could always rely on human behavior to expand the drama.

It was better than any tabloid could invent. People lost control, drew blood, felt and caused pain – all nudged by his Midas touch.

The first domino had been set when the gun was put into Mack's hands. It was plastic, untraceable, and homemade. A computer hacker spit it out on a 3D printer and gave it to the old psychopath biker, with information about the show where Ayla and Moeda would appear.

"Be a man about this," the hacker was told to say.

It cost The Senator ten grand – pennies to him.

After the first domino, it was simple. A few tweaks and the chain reaction kept going, unchallenged. People remained in character, only interested in what they would get for themselves.

Stupid, greedy people. They never caught on – never saw the plot, appreciated the brilliance of his master plan, or heard the dominoes fall.

Particularly this family. He knew them well.

There were a few bugs along the way. She came to his office, fell to her knees, and pleasured him. It was delightful. Then she told him about an occasional domino that refused to fall so he could move it back into place. Paying off Remez to let Mack in and to keep quiet, was costly, but money was never the issue. Mack loved the kill; when he saw the cat, he didn't need any encouragement. That ran in the family, too.

He laughed. The other stuff wasn't all his idea. Just more dominoes falling – threatening texts, ricin scare, blood on the mirror, faked coma. The media cooperated like paparazzi hungering for prey – news reports, blogs, You Tube, and the King of untruths, social media. Beautiful.

Each time she returned to his office, grateful. Power and money on her knees before him. The ratings went up and her intensity increased. It was exhilarating, like sipping a snifter of 20-year old *Louis Royer XO* Cognac.

She amused him with lurid stories – Robert and Sage, Ayla and Mack, Hanya and Steen. All predictable. Moeda.

"Ah, Moeda," The Senator sighed. "She was my political intern – such a fiery kid. Now she's tired and old."

Isobel was another tale. She was a good fuck. He had her first but she preferred Robert over him. Poor choice, but foreseeable. She didn't understand that older men were more skilled. If the pink bitch would have stuck with him, she wouldn't be at Rikers, and Robert wouldn't be dead.

It was a shame that Robert had to die. He would miss him as much as he could miss anyone. Yet Robert was worth the sacrifice for the engrossing plot masterminded by The Senator's God-like abilities.

It *was* a great twist to the story when he made sure Mack met Ayla in Westchester Square Park. It brought back memories of Espie – yet another way to fuck her. The Senator hated the Bronx almost as much as the dead Espie once loved it. He never forgot that Espie had once refused him.

The Senator fingered a single, ivory domino and smiled.

2

The story seemed complete.

Tamirah knocked, and then opened his office door, just as she'd done several times before. She paused, framed by the light behind her. The office was empty. No one *knew.*

A single, white chocolate macaron was on the side table next to The Senator. One for him. None for her. He touched the smooth top, without taking a bite out of the confection.

Boldly, she left the door open, not noticing the macaron. She approached his recliner. "We won," she said breathlessly. "Turn it on." They would watch the show together.

The Senator plucked a domino from the box as he hit the remote and the flat screen TV came to life.

"I always win," he reminded her.

The only time he *didn't* win flashed in his mind. Espie. It was a long time ago, but still lived in his mind.

In those Levittown days, Tamirah was his secret sex slave, but he wanted Espie. She refused him. It was unforgivable. No other woman, before or after, ever refused to fuck him. Even though they were mere adolescents, Espie held the power to reject. The only solution was retribution – perhaps his greatest dominoes plot. Now, Espie was dead – murdered. Only her sister Hanya remained, along with Espie's distasteful granddaughter, Sage. He owned Hanya while Robert had taken care of the red-headed bitch.

The Senator caressed the domino as he and Tamirah stared at the flat screen.

Dr. H stood quietly in front of the studio audience. She wore a new sage-green *Armani* suit, without bloodstains. She patted her hair and faced her fans, a somber expression on her face.

Good choreography, he thought. Makes her believable.

"Welcome to the *New Truth With Dr. H!*" There was a triumphant tone in Hanya's voice. "Today's show is dedicated to Robert, The Senator's Son, who lost his life in pursuit of truth. God bless you, Robert. Rest in peace. Let's take a minute of silence to remember this man whose life was brutally taken from us."

Hanya lowered her head.

There was no movement or sound for ten seconds. Truth. He laughed. The timing was perfect. No one would sponsor a full silent *minute* on the air.

Dr. H raised her head and looked directly into the camera. "My first guests have been invited to discuss what happened *here*, on this show, when truth seemed too difficult to bear. There was a shooting, a death, a psychiatric breakdown, and an escaped attempted murderer."

She paused.

"Let me introduce our guests."

Taped live in New York scrolled across the bottom of the screen. Another truth, The Senator chuckled. Most viewers never realized that the "live" show had taken place earlier – hours, days, weeks? – to make sure everything was safe with no surprises.

"Griet Vansalee," Hanya continued. "Our executive producer – a courageous woman who understood what went on here better than any person on Earth."

Griet appeared, ugly but beautifully coifed and painted, sitting in the chair offered by Hanya.

"And . . ." Hanya continued, "Jake Visch, the attorney who was on the scene and now the star of his new food talk show, *Visch's Vittles*."

There was enthusiastic applause. *Visch's Vittles* had been heavily promoted.

Hanya sat opposite Griet and Visch. "Where did this all begin?" She asked demurely.

The studio audience was dead silent, along with millions of viewers across the country and around the world.

"It began when Mack showed up with his plastic gun," Griet lied. "No one knew he and Ayla plotted to get Moeda's money."

Hanya shook her head. "Poor Moeda. She's the true victim."

"Yes, she is," Griet said sharply.

"Ayla and Mack will never be found," Visch jumped in. "People like that know how to disappear."

"What about the baby? He's grown up – maybe he'll contact the show . . ."

Visch shrugged.

The Senator rubbed the domino in his hand. "It's a shame that Steen and Sage wouldn't go on the show. I made sure Steen received a promotion and Sage's new proposal for her dissertation would be accepted. They don't appreciate my generosity."

A short clip of Isobel in Rikers was aired on the flat screen behind Hanya, followed by a longer trailer from Robert's video. It ended with a still of the pink *Kahr P380* pistol.

"A stunning murder weapon," Tamirah commented.

"Yes," The Senator agreed. "There's a run on those guns. Pity I don't own the stock."

During the commercial break, Tamirah kneeled in front of The Senator. "You did it," Tamirah said. "You're greater than any man."

"Of course."

"Power and money. Ratings off the charts. On my knees."

Tamirah unzipped The Senator's fly.

He closed his eyes. He was getting bored with the kike and her red silicon spiked tongue stud. This would be the last time.

"Thank you. Thank you. Thank you." The Senator sighed.

Tamirah took him into her mouth, rubbing the stud against his erection. The Senator smiled as if they were kids again, hiding in his Levittown bedroom and doing the unthinkable.

Suddenly, Tamirah stopped.

He opened his eyes to see what happened.

"What's wrong?"

Tamirah wasn't looking at him or his penis. Her eyes were on the door that she had left open. He followed her gaze. A woman was framed in the light. He recognized her instantly.

"Sage," The Senator said pleasantly. "Would you like to join us?"

Tamirah giggled.

Sage went rigid. She screamed. Her words shot through the office, like lightning bolts from a Nazi Iron Eagle.

"You. Tamirah. Robert. Mack!"

Why?

Check out the next book in the Broken series:

It's 1992 and a spine-chilling newborn is destined for evil. Who was Joshua and where did he come from? Was Sage really in love with her cousin? What did The Senator have to do with Sage's beloved Grandma Espie?

Available in ebook and print
on amazon.com

Read an excerpt from

Broken By Birth: Book 2

Ayla

1

He was a few hours old and about to be thrown away.

Ayla shuddered. The baby shuddered.

She counted his fingers and toes. She touched his chest to make sure he was breathing and smoothed the caramel-colored down on his head. "You're the prettiest baby in the world."

That's what good Mommas were supposed to say. Ayla wasn't going to be a Momma for very long, so she had to get everything right.

"You're beautiful," she added. "You'll have a very good life."

"Ten minutes," Mack's voice roared through the gloomy basement apartment. He sounded like a Harley revving up for a long trip. Sometimes, Ayla would remember the caramel-and-white colored feral cat she had found on the street. It was a beautiful creature, but lost, just like Ayla. There was sadness in the cat's blue eyes – no one wanted her but Ayla. Like no one wanted the baby in her arms.

Mack appeared, a shadow beneath the crooked, caged industrial light.

The air smelled subterranean – moldy, old, and mildewed. Eerie canned music reverberated through her head. A commuter train thundered nearby, passing through the Freeport Long Island Railroad Station.

They lived in the basement of a crumbling house, behind a factory on Sunrise Highway, and a block south of the railroad tracks. The entrance was in the back, through a sagging fence that was once painted bright blue. A water tower hovered over them like a blue monster stealing the sky. Druggies lived upstairs – she never knew how many - there was a constant flow of people, coming and going, beneath the old white metal awning on the front door. The tenants sold and used everything from heroin to meth. Sometimes there was an eerie quiet; other times music was so loud it hurt her ears.

"Ten minutes," Mack said again, his voice threatening. "Me," Mack pointed to his chest, "not him." He lifted his right hand, curled three stubby fingers into a fist, extended his index finger, and raised his thumb in a simulation of a gun. Grinning, he aimed at the baby's head. "Click."

Mack turned away and everything swirled in hand-held camera action – dizzying distortions on a bigger-than-life screen. Ayla blinked. She was tired and sore, but alive. The day had passed in a blur of pain; a day she would never forget and a day she would never fully remember.

Mack was the answer - the only road out of the basement apartment.

Mack's arms and chest swelled with bulging steroid muscles rippling beneath a sleeveless tee. His thick jeans hung over steel-toed Dr. Martens embedded with shiny silver eyelets. Both arms were covered with tattoo sleeves ending in SS lightning bolts that shot up his neck. On his thigh, the lightning bolts pointed to his penis. The tee covered a shoulder-to-shoulder chest tattoo of a Nazi Iron Eagle, a swastika in its claws, and a blood red eye.

Ayla closed her eyes. She was mesmerized by Mack's Nazi Iron Eagle. What did it say about him? Often, after they had sex, she would lie naked in his arms and trace the outline of the tattoo with her finger. It was like playing with fire - tempting energies that stoked both guilt and excitement. Why would a grown-up man play Nazi? Why did it make her heart pound and her body ache for him?

"You hear me?" Mack snarled. He never yelled; always spoke in frigid monotones.

His voice shocked her back into the present. The Baby. Mack. Click.

"I hear you," she said quickly.

Ayla thought of her mother's favorite song. She softly sang two lines from Patty Smyth's ballad.

There's a reason why people don't stay who they are
Baby, sometimes, love, it just ain't enough.

Read all the books in the Broken Series

Haunted family trees, chilling photo insights, and twisted psychopaths burst into life, blending fact, fiction, and photos into riveting stories you'll never forget.

Books can be purchased in eBooks or print books at: www.amazon.com

Amazon #1 Bestsellers!

Broken By Evil
Return to the 1990s and meet the *real* Joshua. What horrific secrets did Grandma Espie keep from Sage and the rest of the family? How did Joshua carry out his psychopathic legacy? Why did The Senator care? *Book 3*

Broken By Madness
Go back in time to 17th century New Amsterdam and meet the ancestors of Joshua, Sage, Hanya, and The Senator. How does a psychopath terrify an entire community? What does Jew's Alley have to do with Hanya's condo? Who is the Slave Girl and The Indian? *Book 4*

Broken By Men
Plunge into the past to the 1490s and its unspeakable horrors. Trace the legacy of Joshua, Hanya, Sage, and The Senator, as they wander through the brutal, unforgiving streets of Lisbon. *Book 5*

Broken By Kings

Discover the bloody 15th century murder where it all began. Meet the psychopathic soldier, Simao, and follow Esperanza when she was kidnapped and sent to Sao Tome, Africa. *Book 6*

Broken: The Prequel

It's 1492 and the Secret Jewish Tapiador family is betrayed to The Inquisition. Armed soldiers arrive to arrest them. The two daughters escape via a tunnel that leads to safety. The parents are dragged to the torture chambers. Will any of them survive the horrors that pervade Spain?

Books can be purchased in eBooks or print at:
www.amazon.com

Is there a psychopath in your life? Go to http://hauntedfamilytrees.com/haunted-family-trees-landing/ to sign up for your FREE copy of Dr. Fink's ground-breaking guide.

Discover the secrets of haunted family trees – from the infamous to your own . . . Go to http://hauntedfamilytrees.com/haunted-family-trees-landing/ to get stories that will amaze you, the truth in facts and photos, and the latest info about family curses and bizarre behavior.

Do you love photo insights? Go to: http://hauntedfamilytrees.com/landing-page to get a free image each week in your email that will enlighten, inspire, and make you feel good.

Meet the
Book People

Dr. Jeri Fink

Author, Photographer

I was eight years old.

Faces were penny candy – endless shapes and flavors. Colors throbbed in rhythmic neon lights. My world was a rush of stories written in black-and-white composition books.

There were so many ways to *see* things. The Oak outside my window was big and powerful – or shaky, like a typical New York City tree. I could take a sliver of black charcoal and make the same tree magically come alive on paper. My characters moved through plots more animated than the people next door. I aimed my camera and shot images that no one else noticed.

They called me a free spirit.

I wanted to share, but most of my friends were in different spaces. We went to college and they talked about business, teaching, and making money. I wanted to know about art, lucid dreaming, and the human spirit. We grew up, got jobs, and evolved into families. There were spouses and children; Little League and PTA. I had my family, a home in the suburbs, and a family room painted purple. When everyone dined on backyard barbeque, I preferred Chinese noodles. I stashed chocolate fudge brownie ice cream to weather blizzards, and talked about books no one read at the neighborhood dinner parties.

I never quite *fit*.

I went back to school and became a Family Therapist to help people negotiate their lives. I worked with everyone from "normal" to psychopath. My friends thought *I* was crazy.

Oddly, I was always ahead of my time. I played on the internet before most people had ever heard the word. I developed, along with a group of far-reaching thinkers, the idea of psychotechnology – the psychology of technology. My nonfiction book, *Cyberseduction*, was written long before eHarmony and match.com went viral. Donna Paltrowitz and I worked with kids on books where children became a voice in their own literature. We called the series *The Gizmo Books*. Gizmo and his "sister" Coco were Labradoodles – an Australian breed which most people at the time, including the vet, never knew existed.

Instead of simply growing up, my eight year old *evolved*. In the twenty-eight books I've written since then – nonfiction, children's, and adult fiction – I'm still an author with faces, colors, and stories fueling my imagination.

The *Broken Book* series is a culmination of who I am – the voices of those who entered my mind and heart; the people who pass me on different paths with their own haunted family trees; and the photos that tell their stories.

I travel a road of images, stories, and ideas – all with no end.

Welcome to my world.

Visit me at www.hauntedfamilytrees.com

Email me at jeri@hauntedfamilytrees.com

Join my photo insights blog at:

hauntedfamilytrees.com/landing-page/

Join my haunted family trees blog at:

hauntedfamilytrees.com/haunted-family-trees-landing/

Purchase my books at amazon.com

Donna Paltrowitz

Author

I won!

It was a school writing contest for the best autobiography, and mine came in first. I was in the sixth grade and had no clue about writing. The words flowed effortlessly from my head to the pen. The teacher described my essay as an intricate process rich with ideas, humor, and the desire to connect with others.

Years later, I graduated from college, worked as a teacher in Brooklyn, N.Y. and realized that teaching children to express themselves wasn't the seamless process that I had envisioned. This was a different generation with needs that required new techniques and resources. Spending my days in the classroom with children, and nights earning a Master's Degree in reading, I discovered the latest, most effective techniques to make the entire room smile.

I became a reading specialist. My ideas flowed into developing tools to motivate struggling readers. Focusing on real experiences that kids encountered in their schools, streets, and homes, I created a humorous reading series for children with limited reading vocabularies. Along with my husband Stuart, also a New York City teacher, we wrote the *I Hate To Read Series* – 24 books with music, rhymes, and smiles – long before rap and Miss Piggy became a hit.

We connected with children throughout the country and the English-speaking world. Subsequently, we wrote the *Work World Series* for teenagers trying to make sense of their lives. When schools finally wired up, we designed *Computer Crossroads* and *Mystery Mazes*— software series that engaged young people in reading, laughing, and making fun choices.

Watching my own three children grow up, I realized that reading connections continually evolve. While teachers and administrators tried to lead children to relevant topics, kids were more interested in what their peers were saying. Children connected when they were given a voice. Dr. Jeri Fink, my friend, neighbor, and a LI family therapist agreed that children should have the chance to bring their own literature to life. Together we brought children's issues, words, and artwork alive in *The Gizmo Books*. We visited classrooms with Gizmo, a 100 pound therapy dog and his "sister," Coco. The Labradoodles came from Australia, driving their messages to connect children, parents, grandparents, and schools half way around the world.

Meanings of words shift with the passage of time while the human need to connect remains unchanged. What was once called interacting with friends, neighbors, and colleagues, is now social networking—sharing our messages, bonding with others in the world, and helping us all to feel warm and fuzzy on the inside. Both the teacher and child inside me continue to seek new pathways into the present, as well as the past. That is the heart of *The Broken Book Series*-stories rich with ideas, photos, and the desire to connect with others. Whether child or adult, our families bind us to the good, the bad, and the ugly of our histories. Wander through these adult novels for an insightful connection to the haunted family trees that make us who we are.

Visit us at www.hauntedfamilytrees.com
Email me at donna@hauntedfamilytrees.com

Derek Murphy
Book and Cover Designer

Derek Murphy started a book editing company while working on his PhD in Literature, but soon began using his background in fine arts to help clients with their book covers. Derek believes in using art to create an immediate emotional connection with readers, and get them invested in your story before they even open the book. Check out Derek's website at:

www.creativindiecovers.com

book web publishing, ltd.

Book Web Publishing, ltd. was founded in 2000 to provide a forum for creative and unique works in children's and adult literature.

Thanks!

How do you thank everyone who was part of a project that spanned six years, six books, and tens of thousands of photographs? It's a daunting job. If we leave anyone out please forgive us – there was an overwhelming number of people who have been part of our lives and work during the creation of the *Broken Books* series.

First, our families:
    Our husbands, Richard Fink and Stuart Paltrowitz.

Our children and their children:
    Russell, Laura, Mason, and Emma Fink
    Adam & Blair Paltrowitz.
    Darren Paltrowitz and Melissa Andreev
    Shari Paltrowitz
    Stacey, Greg, Johnny, and Nicky Rossi.
    Meryl & Tony Waters.

Our extended families:
Harvey Fink
Robin March
Bruce and Jillian Milman
Ronnie & Sherry Milman
Sandra Roth
Barbara & Chris Woolley

Many thanks to our friends and supporters who listened to our stories, drowned our troubles in chocolate, and were always there when we needed them. Sheryl Ackerman, Jay Braiman, Dr. Barton Cohen, Sheldon Crooks, Cindy DiBiasi, Joyce & Joel Feldman, Dr. Edward Fryman, Pat & Mary Ann Hannon, Howie Hutchinson, Janet & Rich Kam, Dale Kranz, Bill Kumar, Jerry & Jill Lash, Dr. Carol Levy, Joan Mirabella, Gail Orlick, Barbara Saks, John Viollis, and Sandra Weiss.

Special appreciation goes to our readers: Fern Friedman, Laura & Russell Fink, Craig Oldfather, Dr. Sandra Roth – our experts: Nancy Allegretti, Mary Ann Hannon, Margaret Mendel – our designer, Derek Murphy, and our copy editor Pat Hannon.

Thanks to Sue and Ken Yaeger, who generously shared their experiences and insights to bring these books alive.

A tasty thanks to *Chocolate Works of Bellmore-Merrick, La Maison Du Chocolat,* and *Nom Wah Tea Parlor.*

Our gratitude goes to the many artists, authors, filmmakers, investigative reporters, photographers, psychologists, researchers, social workers, theorists, and videographers who informed our work, empowering us to accomplish our mission.

In loving memory of Judy Becker, Dora Eisenstein, Edna Fink, Joseph March, Gladys & Larry Milman, Ruth Roth, Sandra Roth, and Vincent Meo.

Last, but not least, thanks to our readers who joined us in this amazing journey.

Publisher's Note

This is a work of fiction. Names, characters, places, and incidents either are the product of the authors' imaginations or are used fictitiously, and any resemblance to actual persons, living or dead, business establishments, events, or locales is entirely coincidental.

The scanning, uploading, and distribution of the book via the Internet or via any means without the permission of the publisher is illegal and punishable by law. Please purchase only authorized electronic and print editions, and do not participate in, or encourage electronic piracy of copyrighted materials. Your support of the authors' rights is appreciated.

Visit us online at www.hauntedfamilytrees.com